IT'S NEVER OVER

IT'S NEVER OVER

Morley Callaghan

Introduction by
Norman Snider

EXILE
editions

Library and Archives Canada Cataloguing in Publication

Callaghan, Morley, 1903-1990
    It's never over / Morley Callaghan ; introduction by Norman Snider.

Includes bibliographical references.
ISBN 978-1-55096-157-7

    I. Title.

PS8505.A43I8 2011   C813'.52   C2011-907132-0

Design and Composition by Hourglass Angels-mc
Typeset in Times New Roman and New Yorker at the Moons of Jupiter Studios
Printed by Imprimerie Gauvin

This novel is a work of fiction. Names, characters, places and incidents are the products of the author's imagination. Any resemblance to actual persons, living or dead, events, or locales is entirely coincidental.

Published by Exile Editions Ltd.
144483 Southgate Road 14 – GD
Holstein, Ontario, N0G 2A0
Canada   www.ExileEditions.com
Printed and Bound in Canada in 2011

Conseil des Arts   Canada Council
du Canada   for the Arts

Canadä

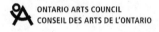

ONTARIO ARTS COUNCIL
CONSEIL DES ARTS DE L'ONTARIO

The publisher would like to acknowledge the financial support of the Canada Council for the Arts, the Government of Canada through the Canada Book Fund (CBF), and the Ontario Arts Council–an agency of the Government of Ontario, for our publishing activities.

Sales / Distribution:
Independent Publishers Group
814 North Franklin Street, Chicago, IL 60610 USA
www.ipgbook.com   toll free: 1 800 888 4741

Contents

Morley Callaghan's Toronto Noir

1.

It was an electrifying time for writing. Morley Callaghan was a rising twenty-seven year-old novelist with a Paris and New York reputation and an instinct for the provocative. He had dealt with incest (*An Autumn Penitent*), lesbianism (*No Man's Meat*), and gang warfare (*Strange Fugitive*.) In 1930, he published, in New York and Toronto, his second novel, *It's Never Over*. Callaghan's darkest book, it is one of the most original of his stories, an extraordinary meditation on sexuality, on possession as an abscess of the spirit, and violence.

This bleak yet exhilarating tale demonstrates that Callaghan stands with the William Faulkner of *Sanctuary* or that "poet of the tabloid murder," James M. Cain, whose *The Postman Always Rings Twice* this novel anticipates by more than a decade.

Callaghan, however, did not miss a tabloid career writing for *Thrilling Detective*; he is no perpetrator of sex and murder pulp fiction; the killing and execution he depicts in *It's Never Over* take place off-stage, at the beginning of the story and the sex he describes is not Faulkner's corncob rape or Cain's "jungle lust," though, in the context of the morality of the times, the candid sensuality of his characters is definitely illicit and has the gravest social consequences. Moreover, the connection he makes between sex and violence places Morley Callaghan in the company of the hard-boiled bunch that Edmund Wilson called "The Boys in the Back Room." Ring Lardner, Cain, John O'Hara, Hemingway, James T. Farrell. Like Callaghan, this crew of writers who emerged in the late 1920s and early 1930s, with one or two exceptions, came from the world of journalism. Their stories came out of combat reporting, the sports world, show biz, and the crime beat.

Newspaper reporters were the day laborers of the intellectual world and proud of it. They shared H.L. Mencken's hostility to cant, piety, and pietistic institutions. They were more than likely to be found in the back rooms of nightclubs and saloons and police stations as they explored the less polite precincts of the culture. Iconoclastic, they did not see themselves as stenographers to the established orders of society.

The novels of this school often emerged from a vanishing staple of newspaper writing, known as "the human interest story," stories fueled by a sense of injustice, outrage at the undeserved fate suffered by an embattled individual. For Morley Callaghan, the ruggedest of individuals himself, a political liberal, and a anarchist in spirit, the individual and the individual's soul were of singular importance in God's creation.

2.

Toronto in the 1920s. The violence of the Great War is a recent and searing memory; the city still reels from its aftershocks. Fred Thompson, a high school friend of the protagonist, John Hughes, is found guilty of murder and is hanged at the Don Jail while a sullen but not unruly crowd mills outside. Thompson, once a high-minded young man, disillusioned by the war in the trenches, had devoted himself to drink, to partying.

Quick to anger, he had killed a policeman who had slugged him in a speakeasy raid, smashing him on the head with a chair.

Where a writer like Cain detailed the beginnings of a relationship that ended up in the electric chair, Callaghan depicts the ruinous moral and psychological effects the murder and subsequent execution have on Hughes, on Fred's sister Isabelle, and on his fiancee Lillian. John Hughes, an aspiring oratorio singer and something of an intellectual who reads Mencken's *American Mercury*, drops Isabelle out of cowardice and snobbery, and starts sleeping with Lillian.

(Callaghan expertly depicts this event in a fresh and quite startlingly matter-of-fact fashion. Hughes announces to Lillian that he wants to "love" her. In the parlance of the time, he means he wants to have sex. She wants to have sex, too, and immediately rents an apartment on the outskirts of the city where neither of them are known and they begin to meet there and make love. Just like that. No moral trepidation. Just the desire to be out of the public eye so that they can be who they want to be, do what they want to do.)

Isabelle, sister to the hanged man, believing herself ostracized from polite Toronto society, instead of retreating to a convent, transforms herself into an apostle of evil and turns her sexuality to destructive ends. After bedding down other men, she seeks out Hughes at his rooming house, imposes herself on him, and succeeds — as she seems to want to — in both costing him his room in a respectable house and his job as a *basso* soloist in a church choir. More and more Isabelle seems in the grip of the imp of the perverse. She informs Lillian of what's happened and Hughes loses her too. Isabelle and Lillian set up an informal cult of two feeding on the memory of the dead Fred; Callaghan implies that the relationship is also lesbian. Believing that Isabelle is bent on destroying both himself and Lillian, Hughes loses control of himself and goes right to the brink of murder but the Toronto weather beats him to it. As her psychic wound, the obsession with the hanging of her brother, has festered, so too has she began to waste away physically, becoming more vulnerable to the natural elements. She dies of pneumonia, a kind of wintering away of the spirit, instead. In a sense, these events all stem from the destruction of Fred's self-respect in the trenches. It's the war that's never over.

Callaghan's attitude is unflinching. "A hanging draws everybody into it," he writes, "It takes hold of some stronger than others. Some are sentimental and some are hard, but they're all crucified in their own way."

3.

Read in a new century, *It's Never Over* — for all its focus on obsession and on the hanging spirit at the heart of the city — exudes period charm. The men wear hard derby hats and winged collars; they carry gold watches in their vest pockets. Professional baseball is played on Toronto Island. Single men room with families. Young couples canoe for enjoyment in the pure waters of Lake Ontario close to a dance hall by the Scarborough Bluffs. There aren't many automobiles: the book's characters either take the streetcar or walk. Folks don't lock their doors at night. Some local landmarks remain: Hart House, St. James Cathedral, the Bloor Viaduct. But Callaghan doesn't overdo the local color in a breast-beating, nationalistic fashion; he just describes what the characters see around them as they move through their lives. His small city on a lake is completely specific yet somehow universal because, as Edmund Wilson writes, what the characters see is "made most effectively to merge with the uncomfortable personal relations, the insoluble emotional problems, the stifled guilt that at last takes possession in the dark lie of an insane fixation."

If Callaghan's stance is unflinching, his prose is not. In a delicately lyrical style, Callaghan distills a potent brand of nostalgic local description. In the era before malls, the characters walk through slush as it melts on the sidewalks in front of the department stores at Queen and Yonge; moonlight glints on the roofs of the garages in the East End, and a cold wind is always blowing up from the Lake.

And it's more than the weather that's chilling.

Toronto is a place rife with intolerance. Here is a chill composure among the people, in their eyes, the way they walk. Little Belfast, a city strained with a palpable tension between Catholic and Orange Lodge Protestants. Hypocrisy is inlaid in the climate. Errington, the Protestant landlord who throws the Catholic Hughes out of his house because of his sexual delinquency is, in a stroke of delicious irony, a dogmatic socialist, a loudmouth "progressive." His belief in a better world doesn't prevent him from making it his business to get in touch with Hughes' Protestant employers and getting him fired. Callaghan calls Errington "really a hard Puritan"; that is to say, a total piece of shit.

Oh, those Presbyterian blues.

The cruel side of social condescension is a theme that informs Callaghan's fiction from *It's Never Over* to *Such Is My Beloved, The Loved and the Lost, The Many Colored Coat* and *A Time For Judas.* For all the expansive and outward feel of his work, *It's Never Over* is totally in tune with Northrop Frye who wrote that Canada is a garrison society; that is, the local gentry are forever looking for a reason to throw the unworthy out of the fort and into the cold. It's a concern Callaghan shares with that other "Irish" writer, John O'Hara. His garrison stories of social disgrace were set amongst the country club cliques of small town Pennsylvania. Callaghan wrote of the humiliations of the aspiring middle class of

Toronto and English-speaking Montreal. Though both novelists' characters are more at risk of social or financial ruin than of violent death, death is likely to follow on the heels of social rejection. In *Appointment in Samarra,* the alcoholic auto-dealer Julian English is a suicide by carbon monoxide. In *It's Never Over*, Isabelle Thompson dies of pneumonia brought on by the self-neglect caused by social ostracism. It is no accident, given their minority status, that this sense of shame and social rejection is felt by Irish Catholic writers on either side of the border.

Callaghan is never more convincing than in just these scenes of humiliation. In O'Hara, the character is likely to be thrown out of a bar; in Callaghan, he or she is liable to be thrown out of their job. But Callaghan's characters, as Max Perkins said to him in a letter, "are true, and interesting not as representatives of certain classes, but as individuals." Callaghan is by far the superior psychologist. He's better able than O'Hara to portray the dark states of mind of his outcasts as they tramp the winter streets. Callaghan approaches the great Russian, Dostoevsky, in his sense of the drama of possession, for Isabelle is possessed by and is pursuing what Jean-Paul Sartre would later describe as a phantom that is an all too real parasite — a parasite within — "like a rat within a rat" — that feeds on her anguish and her weariness until it kills her.

Callaghan's originality is increased by his depiction of the way possession as parasitical social shame moves in the precise fashion of a sexually transmitted disease from the promiscuous Isabelle to John to Lillian. The trio are connected by their bodies, their very flesh in the morbid progress of possession as it traps them in the shadow of death. This is sustained insight of a very high order.

All the same, these characters caught up in such high drama are quiet sinners. John Hughes is a grown-up choir boy, so high-minded he won't stoop to singing popular songs. Rather than dump Isabelle and go on his jolly way, he is forever tied to her by guilt and shame and the ghost-like memory of her hanged brother. Hughes succumbs to her vamp-like charms protestingly, reluctantly. The sexual act that ruins his life is all over in seconds; he doesn't even enjoy himself that much. And when Hughes sleeps with Lillian, at Isabelle's behest, she keeps her fists tightly clenched throughout. In this world, even the damned are inhibited.

Nonetheless, it is just this connection that Callaghan makes between sex and death that creates exhilaration. After all, it is this emotional juncture that unleashed the dark energies of European romanticism from Laclos to Wilde. What's striking is to see the Toronto novelist portraying dangerous, fatal liaisons against the Scots Presbyterian backdrop of the 1920s.

The minor characters impress as well. Father Mason, the whisky priest who walks Fred Thompson to the gallows would do the same for many another doomed prisoner in Callaghan's succeeding novels. In *It's Never Over,* he talks John Hughes out of murdering Isabelle. (Another novelist might have thought of bringing the story full circle by letting Hughes whack the girl and end up in the death row cell formerly inhabited by his friend.) Paul Ross is another victim of both the war and Isabelle's charms. Abandoning his architectural studies, he travels small-town Ontario selling magazines door-to-door on the strength of his tales of the horrors of the trenches, which he has reduced to a Fuller Brush Man's sales' talk. Unlike John Hughes, he can take his pleasure of Isabelle and then just keep on partying.

Callaghan doesn't moralize about such behaviour. As far as he's concerned, Fred Thompson's mortal sin resides solely in his turning his back on his belief in himself as a unique individual as a result of his experience of the mass slaughter of the war. His death and his sister's are a direct result of his abandoning his own self-respect. The only other character who proposes a similar denigration of the individual is the Communist John Hughes encounters in a seedy rooming house after he's been thrown out by the respectable Eddington. Hughes is infuriated when the guy enunciates his theory of the paramount important of the masses over any individual existence. One senses that Callaghan shares his rage. It is the collective opinion of respectable Toronto that has destroyed Hughes' life.

As for Callaghan's resemblances to and parallels with writers like Cain, Farrell, and O'Hara, it's possible to push too far. As a writer, he was his own man almost to the point of solipsism. His characters are far more reflective and genteel than Cain's or Farrell's, and not as grand and socially glib as O'Hara's. John Hughes is no Studs Lonigan and he is passive compared to the general run of *noir* protagonists, yet he compels our interest.

The sensibility of the novel is essentially Christian and forgiving. Not only does Callaghan not condemn Hughes and Isabelle for their sexual transgressions, he depicts them with an extraordinary compassion. For the embattled individual, Callaghan has nothing but sympathy. He is permanently on the side of the lone soul, even if the lone soul is damned and condemned by all of society. Callaghan offers Isabelle as a kind of inverted martyr; Father Mason is the only man in the city who understands this but his Church has no satisfactory response; his only recourse is drink.

In the last words of the novel, the cityscape and the emotional landscape merge in an exceptional bit of writing as Callaghan uses the Toronto climate to symbolize the final distance between his characters:

"They were at the corner where the car stopped. The wind was blowing and Lillian was holding her hat with one hand and her coat with the other. A car was coming and they went to speak, but the wind carried the words away. It was such a cold wind it was more important Lillian should not miss the car than they should go on talking."

4.

Callaghan's novel is a book with a relevance that is not only peculiarly contemporary but of perennial value. All ages and all generations must deal with death and tragedy whether as a result of war or terrorism or the garden variety disaster that visits all of us at one time or another. The sentimentality of the Victorians has been replaced by a therapeutic sentimentality that asks for "closure." Morley Callaghan's novel refutes this Wal-Mart optimism, this forlorn hope that one can "move on" from a devastating, tragic event such as a brother's hanging and emerge from it innocent once again, without scars. There are some things in life so awful that they stay with you forever. It's Callaghan's belief that the only remedy is a kind of unflinching hope that faces up honestly to despondency and even despair. Time moves on but the hanging is never over, in the heart.

Norman Snider, Toronto

CHAPTER ONE

A crowd was gathering outside the wall by the park, when the streetcar he was on, coming home from work, curved along the avenue on the hill. His legs started to twitch as he tried to turn away, but like everybody else he pressed his face against the window, waiting for the car to turn at another angle so he could look back at the crowd.

He sat there calmly, feeling the pain in his neck from craning. The car stopped three times and people got off. He could stand the tension of this calmness no longer, and getting up suddenly got off just before the doors closed. He walked back rapidly the way of the car tracks, and kept on cracking his fingers, pulling every one in turn until the knuckles cracked, and he avoided looking far along the street past the curve to the jail.

An iron fence was alongside the walk all the length of the park, and on the other side of the fence the hill sloped down to the flatland, rolled and hard and green. The greenest, tightly clipped grass was on the bowling lawn at the foot of the hill and on the tennis court, but beyond were pools of water in the spongy ground. The surface of the pools shone in the bright sunlight and the sky was very blue. John Hughes, walking on the sidewalk on the hill, kept on looking down at the flatland, following with his eyes as he walked, four tennis players on the public courts early in the evening, the two girls wearing red bandeaux.

The crowd was hidden by the trees in the park. He broke into a trot, breathing heavily, afraid that if he did not get there soon the mob would disperse, and he simply wanted to be one of them, outside the jail, gaping at the window of the death-cell high up on the wall. In the morning they were hanging Fred Thompson, who had been his friend for many years, and he was eager to be in the crowd because the presence of so many people outside the jail, staring at the cell window, created a contact with the man in the cell. Anyone there was closer to Fred Thompson than John would have been if he had gone home and had his dinner and put his hands over his face, still thinking about him; but if the crowd dispersed, then the tension and excitement would be all gone and only the foolish ones would stand alone in the park underneath the trees. So John Hughes went on running, eager to get the feeling there was for him in the crowd.

Looking back once he saw that even the tennis players had left the court and were climbing the hill quickly, swinging their rackets. The white shirts and trousers of the men looked very nice moving along the green hill.

He eased up in his stride, just walking rapidly, mopping his forehead with his handkerchief, and more excited inside than he had been when he first got off the car, though he did not know what he expected to happen among the people, who had come from all the side streets.

A lane was between the wall of the jail and the iron fence at this end of the park. It was an old jail and the wall was not very high, hardly more than twelve feet, and people standing a few yards from the park fence could look over the jail wall at the narrow barred windows in the weather-browned brick of the jail.

The people standing under the trees were staring at the cell window, pointing, talking rapidly without looking at each other. There had been a sun shower an hour ago and the leaves on the trees were still wet and sometimes drops of water from the leaves fell on someone's head. The light from the strong sun glistened on the surface of the wet leaves through the trees, but could not dry the soggy ground, heel-marked and trampled. A broad-shouldered man, his arms linked behind him, standing on tiptoes, suddenly shouted: "There he is!"

The outline of Thompson's face was behind the three bars of the window. The white face was pressed against the bars. It was really too far away to see whether the face was white, but it was a pale blotch against the shadow of the cell window. When everybody understood a face was at the window they began to cheer a little uncertainly, because they had followed his trial and felt sure that if he hadn't killed a policeman he would have been given only life imprisonment. The weak cheering irritated three policemen on horseback in the land between the park and the jail wall, and slapping their horses they jerked the reins till the horses pawed the ground, swinging back on their haunches almost in a circle. There was no more cheering, but someone in the center of the crowd yelled at the policemen and everybody laughed. John Hughes, moving nervously in the crowd, shouldering people aside, had seen the face at the window, and it no longer was necessary to keep on looking at it; now he wanted to be moving in the crowd, irritating people standing on tiptoe, whom he tilted off balance. Suddenly he stopped, remaining quietly on the one spot by the tree trunk, wondering what so many faces in the park meant to the man in the cell. All the faces were lifted to him, and now he was pressing his own face against the bars as if it had become very important that he should not miss a single movement or fail to see a single upturned face. The eager movements, the faces lifted up to him and the small cheer were the movements and rhythm in a brief new world, important in every detail because he had an immediate relation with everything in it. Everything for the moment belonged to him. The face never moved behind the bars, and was always turned at the same angle, neck craning toward the crowd, and John felt like crying as he looked intently at the man nearest to him, a tall thin man with a short dark beard, hoping to recognize instantly some quality so sympathetic to his own mood he could take hold of him by the arm and start talking. The man's long face was absolutely expressionless, only his eyes never wavered. Timidly, John reached out his hand, hardly touching the thin man on the arm. "What's the matter with you?" the man said, glaring at him. The bearded jaw moved abruptly three times, the man blinked his eyes rapidly, again concentrating on the cell window and John was no longer anxious to feel all the eager emotion of the crowd. On the street a peanut vendor with a pushcart was trying to adjust the handle of the cart against the iron fence so he could stand up on it and look over the jail wall. A policeman took him by the arm, shaking him. John, looking a long time at the peanut vender and at the policemen and at the streetcars moving on the tracks, and through the leaves of the trees up at the sky and at the faces around him, hoped, when he looked again at the cell window, the face would be gone. It was always there. The face never moved, only it was harder to see it now because the window was on the east wall of the jail and the sun was going down. The window was hardly more than a dark shadow, but the last strong sunbeams were shining on the people on the hill. The feeling he had been eager for, running down the street, had passed; it had been just a short, quick feeling of a unity with tense-faced people and the one in the cell, but the tall man with the narrow bearded face had spoiled it, and he wanted to get out of the crowd, for he was thinking of the high-school years with Fred Thompson, suddenly feeling so sentimental he kept rubbing his hands over his cheeks. He got out of the crowd slowly, moving farther back into the park, and was angry at the ones who had started to sing a song everybody used to sing in wartime. He, too, wanted to sing.

Than he saw Father Mason, a tall and broad-shouldered, moon-faced man, pacing up and down beyond the fringe of the crowd, glancing always at the ground. Beads of perspiration were on his upper lip.

"Mind company, Father?" John asked him.

"Good evening, John."

Slowly they walked along the crest of the hill. Down on the flatland some kids were playing with a football, but it was getting too dark to follow it. The dark oval shape sometimes rose up high against the skyline. The sun had struck the tops of the poplar trees that lined the Don River, running through the whole ravine, now tinting roofs of houses on the other side.

"Why on earth are they singing over there?" Father Mason said.

"I don't know. I guess it holds them together."

"I suppose so. Curious the way they came here tonight. Why on earth did I, too, walk by here? I saw poor Fred this morning."

"Let's sit down here on the bench."

"Very well. But it is wonderful the way he was this morning. You know I've walked to the gallows with three men, but Fred will be the first one that I actually knew. That makes a difference."

"How's he going to take it, Father?"

"Good Lord, he'll die a perfect death. He's absolutely resigned about it. That's the main thing. That's what I have to do. He wasn't a very good Catholic, not like his sister Isabelle, or his mother, but you know he's as simple about it now as a child."

"I can't imagine Fred feeling that way about it."

"That part of it's easy. That's my job. But it makes a difference when you know them. You believe that, don't you?" He spoke childishly, leaning closer to John Hughes. He had had a drink of whiskey, and it was strong on his breath.

"I thought I'd take a walk tonight," he said, "and have everything easy in my mind for tomorrow, but I know why I walked up here."

"So he's easy in his thoughts, is he?"

"He's ready. I walked up here an hour ago."

"So Fred's ready to die. Maybe that's why he never moved his face from the window. I thought he might cry out, shout something to someone in the crowd."

"He's looking forward to it. I try to get them feeling that way. It almost hypnotizes them. He's perfectly reconciled to everything. He's ready to leave the world."

"Good God, Father, it sounds bad thinking of him wanting to die."

"None of them want to die. The bad part will come as he sees the noose. He'll start and straighten up and I can almost see him doing it. Then he'll go on and die a perfect death."

"Let's stop talking about it."

"I didn't even want to think of him tonight."

It was almost dark now and the crowd was dispersing, because they could no longer see the window. Groups of fellows were walking along the cinder path in the park to cross the bridge over the river, the fellows talking rapidly and excitedly, and passing under a light; their faces, raised, were illuminated and ruddy, and someone laughed out loud.

So they sat quietly on the bench at the top of the hill and had their own thoughts, and the east side of the park became tranquil and there were only small sounds. And when it was dark all the lights on the hills on the other side of the valley were in lines forming patterns, and farther up the valley lighted cars moved slowly over the viaduct. Before midnight the sounds in the park had a different co-ordination than in the daytime. Figures moved in the shadows on the hill, and couples sat on all the benches and some lay down on the grass, but on the other side of the river, up the hill, was the zoo, and some of the animals cried out. Down by the river a chorus of boys' voices sang softly and in the quiet park the sound was carried up the hill. Railway tracks ran alongside the river, and far up the river beyond the viaduct a freight train hooted. Coming up the hill, four girls and four boys, arms linked, talked in whispers, some of them laughing, and John Hughes, who knew the park, sitting beside Father Mason, waited to hear more familiar sounds. As soon as the lights went on, forming the patterns on the hill, he listened eagerly for all the sounds belonging with the pattern, and smelled the dampness of the dew coming up from the flats.

"The people in the park now seem very happy," Father Mason said suddenly.

"It's almost the same every night at this hour."

"I hadn't noticed it before."

"When Fred and I were kids we used to come around here a lot."

"What's that?"

"I said, when Fred and I were kids . . ."

"Have you seen his sister, Isabelle, recently?"

"About a week ago."

"I worry about her. I don't worry so much about her mother."

"I saw Isabelle about a week ago. I don't know what to say to her. Half the time she's praying and other times she is sullen and won't speak to anybody. She doesn't expect anyone to speak to her."

"She shouldn't neglect herself the way she does. She hardly bothers to make herself look decent. She's got thin. She's not strong. She's been sick, run down. Didn't she used to go around with you?"

"We thought we felt that way, but six months ago we forgot all about it, after Fred was arrested. She thought she ought to lose everything. It was kind of hard. It was better for both of us."

"I thought about her last night a lot," Father Mason said. "I worry about her."

"His mother won't cry at all tomorrow."

"No, she went through all that."

"I'd go around there tonight, but I don't know what to say to either of them."

"Don't do it. Tell me, John, can you smell whiskey on my breath?"

"A little, not much."

"Then I'll walk home. I oughtn't to take it, but I have got to keep on going. I take too much of it, that's the trouble.

"Nonsense."

"Yes, I do. I mean I oughtn't to take any more tonight because of tomorrow. It bothers me taking it to help over a crisis. I think I'll be going now."

They were walking toward the streetlights, and a nighthawk was screeching overhead. On the sidewalk Father Mason, wiping perspiration off his upper lip, said: "I won't be seeing you tomorrow?"

"No."

"I'll be there in the morning with Isabelle and her mother. Are you coming to the funeral?"

"Lord, the funeral. Fred over there at that window and we're talking about burying him in two days."

"That's the way it is, but I'm used to it."

"I'm coming to the funeral."

"That's good. His mother will like it."

"Good-night, Father."

"Good-night, John."

John, walking home, watched all the stars come out and was glad he was alone, because no one could have shared the desolation of his mood, and all the time, walking, he was assuring himself he was having no thoughts at all.

He lived with a respectable family on a street not far away from the park, only farther up the hill. His room, on the north side of the house, had three wide windows, and when he went upstairs he pulled down the blinds, lying for a long time on the bed. Before coming home he usually had his dinner in a restaurant near the corner, but tonight he had no hunger. Mr.

and Mrs. Errington, who owned the house, were not in, and only small sounds from the street disturbed him.

Fred Thompson had been his friend, though he had not seen him often during the last year. In the war Fred had been a captain, but afterward had not been successful because he had gone to the war too young. He had been having a drink with some friends in a speakeasy and the police had come in and Fred had quarreled with one who had shoved him too roughly and the policeman, using his baton, had slugged him. Fred had cried out and had beaten the officer, hitting him with a chair and had killed him. It was clear to John, who had it all like a bright picture in his thoughts, and often he had talked about it with Father Mason, an old friend of the Thompson's, whose parish work included the duty at the jail. So John lay on the bed in the dark till he began to remember days when he had thought Isabelle Thompson beautiful, and then getting up quickly turned on the light and got a book from the cupboard; a few plays by Synge, for he was reading *The Shadow in the Glen*. Though he knew it was beautiful it could not interest him at all, and he kept on reading the same page many times; the images coming to him from the book were always destroyed by the force of his own images, and he had to start the page over again.

The Erringtons came in. He heard them moving downstairs and he wanted to go to sleep. A bottle of whiskey was in the dresser drawer and taking it out he poured himself a drink, then two more drinks, until he could lie on the bed and feel only his head going around, and by concentrating on that motion he fell asleep.

CHAPTER TWO

*I*n the morning John got up at five o'clock, when the light was all from a blue-gray sky. The dawn always came early, but there was never any sunlight in the east until after seven o'clock. He sat in the back sunroom, looking out over the roofs of the houses sloping down to the lake, and over the parkland to the office towers tipped by the dawn light. The east sides of the slate roofs were a pastel shade and other sides were shadowed, and when the light was stronger the slate roofs and the painted shingles were tilted surfaces of green and crimson and pearl-gray and brown, the surfaces slanting to the sun at sharp angles. And in the garden, leaves on the tall stems of the hollyhocks by the rod fence drooped damply waiting for light.

Fred Thompson was hanged at five o'clock in the morning when there was hardly any light in houses on the streets, because it was daylight saving time. The hangman did his work creditably, but all the prisoners in the jail howled at the minute of the hour, but not because they loved Fred Thompson; the prisoners always hollered when one of them took the short walk to the gallows, and the hangman couldn't get used to it and hated to hear them.

Before the Erringtons were up John went down to the corner and got the paper to read about the crowd that had gathered outside the jail last night. On the street he tried to read but the words were all blurred. It was not because he was excited. Everything in the paper seemed familiar to him, for he had imagined it happening that way, and knew everything would be done perfectly.

He had breakfast in the morning with the Erringtons before going downtown to work. Though fairly well paid as bass soloist at St. Mark's, a wealthy congregation, and sometimes singing over the radio, he had been working in a department store, saving money to have his voice trained in another country. It was not good for him, being in the store, because he had to work too often in the evenings, training his voice and singing at the church, and he was leaving the job at the end of the week, though worried about losing the salary.

At breakfast Mrs. Errington, a plump-faced jolly woman, saw the paper and the picture of Thompson and said: "I guess they hanged the poor fellow this morning."

"They did all right," he said.

"You were a friend of the family, weren't you?" Mr. Errington said. He was a tall thin man, bald and red-faced, a social democrat and a good strong talker.

"Yes, what about it?" John said, looking at him suspiciously, almost expecting to be treated with contempt because he was a friend of the Thompson family.

"Nothing at all," Mr. Errington said. "I just mentioned it."

"Is there anything wrong with it?"

"No. No. Not at all. I don't believe in capital punishment myself. I don't believe that the State should expose itself to the feeling of degradation, and every citizen gets it when he reads the papers about it." He went on talking strongly, offering many familiar opinions, talking judicially, moving his fork carefully on the white tablecloth to illustrate all the points, till Mrs. Errington said: "The poor young man. It's his family that will feel it."

"That is it. That's it," John said quickly.

"Don't you want to listen to me?" Mr. Errington said indignantly, though not really angry, for he knew both John and his wife had heard the same opinions many times; he simply wanted to go on talking, and when they were not paying attention, he shrugged his shoulders and began using his fork on his food instead of marking the tablecloth in neat lines.

On the way to work on the streetcar, John pressed his face against the windowpane, passing the jail in the corner of the park.

In the store, moving easily in the aisles, he was polite at first to all the customers, but later in the morning he hardly answered them, leaning idly against a counter, thinking of Fred's sister, Isabelle, and of his mother and the funeral and all the words he ought to use speaking to them, and it was not easy to find any combination of words. The pictures in his mind of Isabelle and the man with his face pressed against the barred window became too blurred and he tried to blot them out with happy thoughts of his own girl, but it was difficult, so he looked around suddenly at other salesmen whose faces were like those he had seen in the crowd last night, only now without tension or excitement in them. The street doors opened and bargain-hunters rushed along the aisles; he saw all the faces again and was first uneasy, then ready to vomit, and severely critical of any plan that had ever induced him to work in the store, for he could at least live on the money he got singing in the churches. He began to laugh to himself and kept on laughing when the manager passed along the aisle. The whole department seemed to amuse him suddenly, now he knew he was quitting the job at the end of the week. At noon, punching his card at the time-clock in the basement, he was happier than he had been all morning, a few minutes of a happy feeling, thinking mainly of leaving behind most of the thoughts of the last few months. He was smiling, walking along the street to Martin's Cafeteria. He walked erectly, leaning back on his heels, raised with a cork insole to add an inch to his height, because his music teacher had said that a man with such a good bass voice ought to be a little taller. It was warm on the streets at noon-time, one of the last warm days in September, and in two weeks everybody would be wearing light overcoats. The bright colors of the girls' dresses on the street and glossy tinted silks draped in big store windows helped him hold this simple feeling of happiness.

After lunch he walked over to the small square at the old gray church of St. James, with the iron chains on the concrete walls around it, and taking a newspaper from his pocket, spread it out on the grass and lay down to wait for Lillian. The grass was thick and green and the sunlight was on his face. His hat was tilted over his eyes and he was feeling peaceful and the grass was cool and everything quiet: all the usual downtown noises were there but belonging to the peacefulness of the moment. There were no strange, sharp noises. Out of one eye, from underneath the hat, he was looking across the street at the ochre front of a store and the red side of a bread wagon, waiting for Lillian to come through the gate.

He saw her and got up and sat on the bench, smiling. She was a small, slim woman with very fair hair; her face fresh and cool, but her eyes, a little too big, expressing every fugitive feeling easily. As soon as she was beside him she sat down quickly and started to tremble, her face pale, her eyes blinking. She was Isabelle Thompson's friend and had walked in the evenings with Fred and had gone to the theater with him before she had come to love John Hughes.

"I'm going to quit my job," he said at once.

"What's that?"

"I'm going to quit my job."

"Yes, I know."

"At the end of the week."

"Yes."

"Because it's ridiculous of me to be working in that store. I hate the place. Why do I need to do it?" He tried to go on talking about the store, working himself up slowly, ready to be violently angry, but was only staring at her. She said suddenly, "Poor Fred. Poor Fred. They killed him this morning."

They had been trying to avoid mentioning it, and vaguely it occurred to him that possibly he was talking about the job so they would not have to talk about Fred Thompson. For a few minutes he had been happy and away from it, lying on the grass, and now he was drawn back again, and they sat close together on the bench, each waiting for the other to start talking. Lillian began to speak of Isabelle and then cried quietly, trying to put her head down on John's shoulder. He didn't answer her. First he thought it was beautiful that Lillian should be so sympathetic for Isabelle, and loved her for her nervous, fine feeling, but suddenly he resented so much sympathy for Isabelle alone. Lillian was powdering her nose, pushing her fair hair back under her hat. Two of the bums, who were always stretched out on the grass at noontime, stared at them lazily. Farther up the street, a block away, in the Methodist church the carillon bells began to ring out rapidly. John got up from the bench, for it was time to go back to work. They walked up Yonge Street together as far as the department store.

"Will you do some radio work?" she said.

"I hope so. Stanton, at the church, will get me more."

"I thought you didn't like it."

"I don't. I'd rather do some concert work in the small towns with you."

"I'd like it, doing it together, in the towns."

"You're so good at the piano it helps me out."

"No. I have only facility; you've got something else. You must go on, whatever happens."

"I'm going on. I've got to go on."

"As a pianist I'm not much better than Isabelle."

"You are indeed."

"No. When she used to play for you she did it so sympathetically it sounded beautiful."

"I guess so."

"She hardly plays at all now, hardly touches the piano."

"Please let us stop talking about her."

"We ought to. It seems recently we've always been talking about Isabelle."

At home in the evening, Mrs. Errington handed him a letter he read going slowly upstairs. It was from Mrs. Thompson, though in Isabelle's handwriting, and she wanted him to sing at the requiem high mass she was having for Fred at the church. It was a dignified letter, but she was eager that someone who had been friendly with Fred should have a part in the service. She said it would be necessary for him to see Father Brody at the parish church and say he would help to sing the mass. They were burying Fred in the morning at nine o'clock and expected only a few friends would come to the house and then to the church. The old lady was determined to make it a decent honorable burial, but John was confused, because he hadn't been in a Catholic church for ten years and had almost forgotten the music; then he remembered that after all Fred had probably died a good Catholic death, so it didn't matter much how he died. It was a splendid idea and splendid of the mother to go through with it, so he was ready to phone the Thompsons' house and agree to sing at the service. The old lady had been fond of his voice years ago before it had become full bass and had resented him singing in Protestant churches, though agreeing he was entitled to be paid as highly as possible for his work.

He looked through his trunk, among his books, for a Catholic prayer book, but couldn't find one. He thought he ought to read about the service.

Going out he walked over the bridge and called at Father Brody's house, telling the priest Mrs. Thompson had asked him to sing at the mass. The priest was friendly and didn't want to talk about Fred Thompson at all, making it clear it was just another burial of a man who had died a good death at peace with the church and God. And then he phoned the girl who played the organ, asking her to meet John in the church in half an hour, to help him with two or three parts in the mass for the dead. The girl met John and played the organ for him, helping him, but was eager to talk about Fred Thompson; thinking about him, sitting at the organ, her eyes were moist.

Chapter Three

---

*T*he Thompsons lived in a three-storied red-brick house, with a few feet of lawn and a flower garden for a back-yard. The house was always freshly painted and the front lawn well watered and carefully trimmed. A small wire fence was around the lawn at the sidewalk.

Three people, standing on the sidewalk staring at the crepe on the door, turned away and three kids crouched in the alleyway, hiding, when John went up the steps to the front door. He walked into the front room, where the coffin with one tall, thick candle burning at the head was across the corner of the room. The front window shade was down, the candle was the only light, and the room was all shadowed. Three people were sitting on chairs at the curtained door lead-ing into the other room and one, Fred Thompson's mother, a short, plump woman with white hair knotted on the top of her head, came over and shook hands with John. He hardly knew how to answer her for the candlelight flickered and it was hard getting used to the shadows, so he held her hand tightly to express an intimate sympathy, looking at her somberly. Her face was absolutely calm as she looked at him directly and openly, her eyes narrowing a little, seeking for some expression in his face, which might offend her. Her face was pale but calm, and he would rather have done anything in the world at the moment than suggest he did not think her son was being buried just as if he died naturally. She did not expect this attitude from all people, just the few in the room who would be close to her during the day.

Isabelle was sitting with Lillian in the other room. It was almost a week since he had seen her, and he could hardly help hesitating before speaking, her face was so pallid and her hands, fingering a rosary, so thin, and he wondered why he noticed her hands particularly. She always had been a plump girl, standing erect, her back arched, her face highly colored, her thick, black hair combed straight back from her forehead, and she was like that in the days when they had gone riding in the groves in High Park, or gone to the Island to see the ball games and had sat on the rocking chairs on the back lawn under the grapevine in the evening, when all the flowers were blooming and there was a strong scent from rose bushes near the fence. Now she stood up a little too brusquely. All her movements were too jerky now, as though she didn't know whether to be resentfully dignified and aloof from everybody in the room or calm in her acceptance of her brother's death. Standing there, hardly having an opportunity to touch her hand before she withdrew it, he felt that sorrow was too mixed up with other feelings.

"Dear Isabelle," he said.

"It was good of you to come, John."

"Why do you say that? It was not good of me."

"Only one of our relatives came."

He looked around, but could see no one else in the room but Lillian.

"An aunt. She's in the kitchen talking to Ed."

"Who is Ed?"

"A friend of mine. But Aunty, the good woman, oughtn't to have come. She is sitting in there crying, and she's not crying for Fred, but she's crying because she's related to us and doesn't know what to do about it. She just had to come, she said. I took hold of her by the arm and warned her if she bothered Mother at all I'd kill her. Thank God, we've always you and Lillian anyway."

"That's right."

"The two of you are in my thoughts all the time. I don't know what I would do sometimes if I didn't have you to think about."

"Well, it's over now and you'll be happier."

"No, it's not over."

"But you'll be happier from now on."

"No, it's not over, but with you and Lillian, we'll make it easier for each other."

Mumbling words, he hardly answered her, looking down at the toecaps on his boots. Frowning, he heard neither Lillian nor Isabelle talking, for he was bothered by her possessive notion and did not want either Lillian or himself to go on being one with her in the bitterness of her thoughts.

When Isabelle went into the front room he said to Lillian: "Who is this Ed?"

"He's not very nice, but he's been seeing a lot of Isabelle the last few months."

"But who is he?"

"He played ball with Fred three years ago, and goodness knows how he started going with Isabelle."

The aunt, a wide-hipped tall woman, moving heavily, daubing her eyes with a small handkerchief, came into the room and behind her Ed moved reluctantly, a stocky man with ill-fitting clothes, who did not know what to do with his hands and so kept fingering one fist, then the other. His winged collar and black tie looked simply ridiculous, exasperating John so much he cleared his throat rapidly, staring coldly at Ed, who seemed glad to find someone at all interested in him. He smiled, letting all the expression go out of his face quickly to show an exhaustion from his own sorrow, but could hardly conceal his excitement.

"Did you know Freddie well?" he asked.

"I did."

"We palled around a lot, too, and there he is in there. Like that, too. Can you beat it? Can you beat it?"

"I don't want to think about it."

"Me neither. Only I could tell you hundreds of stories about Fred if we get talking about him."

Father Mason came in and shook hands with Mrs. Thompson and moved restlessly the length of the room. His face was extraordinarily red. People spoke to him, but he only shook his head and would not talk because he wanted to re-main absolutely composed. When he first came in he had spoken briefly to Mrs. Thompson, standing in the hall, and after that he would not even sit down. Three times he looked directly at John, hardly recognizing him, though finally he nodded and said: "Good morning, John."

"Good morning, Father."

"Well.."

"It looks a little like rain."

"Fred . . . .."

"He died a fine death. He died beautifully. I never saw anything like it. Listen, John, tell Mrs. Thompson and Isabelle that I had to go, will you? I have to get back to the church. I have to go at once."

He shook hands with John and Lillian and went quietly.

It was time to move the casket over to the church, and five men, old neighbors, had come in to help Ed carry the casket. The men looked at the face in the casket, but John would not do it. Two of the neighbors, a short, nervous man with a thick gold watch-chain and a thin man with unnaturally white false teeth, were anxious to move rapidly and get out of the house. They carried the casket out of the house and down the steps to the hearse, sliding it in easily.

The mourners sat in two automobiles behind the hearse. The six pallbearers were sitting together in the first one; John squeezed tightly in the back seat with the short, nervous man, and Ed, could not move his arms freely. The nervous neighbor kept taking out his heavy gold watch, looking as if it had become suddenly important that they get there in a hurry. No one spoke. They were all embarrassed, avoiding a discussion.

The church, only five blocks away, was old, with a large dome, and the entrance far back at the side, a church everybody in the neighborhood liked because it had been built in sections in different periods and was really part of the land and the neighborhood. The six pallbearers carried the coffin to the door, placing it on an iron-wheeled table so they could push it up toward the altar. The feet were pointing toward the altar. The church was dimly lighted, only the flickering altar candles were at all bright, and a few people were in the pews. The mourners followed the casket, wheeled slowly by the pallbearers up the center aisle toward the altar.

John went up the narrow staircase to the gallery and spoke to the young lady at the organ. Five schoolboys were there to sing the mass for the dead. The girl shook hands with John and said that she had explained to the boys the parts he was going to sing.

The requiem mass in the early morning with only a few people in the church was solemn and simple. The few mourners were in pews at the right of the aisle close to the altar rail and the priest, moving silently on the altar carpet in his black-and-silver vestments, sang in the old, tired, aloof voice and the small soprano voices of the boys answered him. John, standing in the balcony, alternately looking at the white, smooth faces of the boys and the small crowd huddled together at the front of the church, was trying to avoid dealing with the notion making him restless and excited, the feeling that he ought not to sing at all or become part of the ceremony or have a part in the sorrow and all the consequences of the death. Breathing easier, his hands, which had gripped tightly the railing, relaxed, as it occurred to him that it was better to be up there in the gallery, sympathetically standing apart and not drawn into it, than down at the altar with Isabelle and her mother and Lillian. So finally, in his turn, he sang easily and with new dignity, his bass voice filling the empty church. A few people in the pews turned around, craning their necks, looking up at him. Waiting to sing again he glared down at the people, resenting their curiosity and refusing to admit to himself that even if it had been a normal Sunday mass and they had heard a new voice they would have turned and looked up at the gallery. The two parts of the mass he sang were not at all familiar, but the music was simple and the organist, satisfied, smiled at him eagerly. On the altar the priest had put on a black-and-silver cape and with two boys holding back the ends, advanced toward the coffin, sprinkling it with the holy water.

John shook hands with the organist and went downstairs when the pallbearers were wheeling the casket out to the hearse.

A crowd was on the steps when they carried the casket out, pressing around them tightly, peering at the casket. It was hard moving freely toward the sidewalk. A newspaper photographer was trying to get a picture of the small procession moving toward the hearse, and John, looking back, saw Isabelle and Lillian duck their heads, hold each other's arm tightly, but the mother walked straight ahead, her white face so composed the crowd backed away from her, and even the photographer touched his hat, though irritated because it was a dark, dull day, very bad for newspaper photographs. It looked like rain, for the sun had not come out all morning. Before they had gone into the church the sun had been hidden behind thin gray clouds, but now the sky was dark, unbroken, and heavy. The undertaker had provided a small car to take the priest up to the cemetery.

The ride up Yonge Street was short, there was hardly any traffic, and it was a straight road ahead. The cemetery was almost at the city limits, in the new district, with many fine houses on one side of the street and old frame houses on the other. As soon as they got out of the cabs John walked ahead to stand beside Lillian, afraid she would be hurt too much by Isabelle's sorrow.

They buried Fred Thompson among the newer graves extending down the slope of the hill, away from the older plots in the cemetery with pretentious tombstones and the fine vaults on the flatland at the top. The grass was trimmed and watered on the flatland, but down the hill they had to keep clearing the brush and cutting the weeds, for the tall grass extended right up to the plot where they buried Fred Thompson beside his father. At the head of the plot was a square slab of granite with a stone cross, planted in the top surface. In the last days of September, on the damp, cold day with a few drops of rain falling, the wind blew the last leaves off the trees on the hill, scattering them over the neatly trimmed lawns of the plots. The leaves blew all over the slope and the drier leaves were carried farther away over the flatland and against the vaults.

The priest read the burial service over the empty grave. Fresh earth, clay on top of light-colored sand, was back a way from the pit and a few lumps of clay dislodged by drops of rain fell in quietly and a sudden gust of wind tossed leaves against the earth. The coffin was on the straps, and rollers were letting it down slowly. Mrs. Thompson began to cry quietly and Isabelle put her arm around her shoulder. John, leaning forward intently as they lowered the coffin, was suddenly glad it was disappearing from sight, and anxious for it to be lowered more rapidly and the earth piled in on top. The priest's voice was sounding the words slowly and solemnly and unhurriedly, an old priest with long thin strands of hair who had buried many men in this cemetery. John wanted the earth piled in and the sod pounded over, ending it so he would have no more uneasy thoughts, and had a sudden feeling that if the earth would slide in rapidly at that moment he would never have to think of Fred Thompson again.

The priest had come to the part in his prayers where he reached down with a small trowel and tossed a little earth on the coffin. The earth fell on the casket with a sudden hollow sound, absolutely unexpected and startling, and falling on the casket it reminded John of lumps of earth falling from the roof in the dark cave Fred and he had made up in the bush when they were kids, and after school lumps of earth from the imperfect roof fell into the damp cave, sometimes in their faces and down their necks, while they sat there preferring the mystery of the chilly darkness to the sunlight outside shining through the leaves of the trees. And Isabelle, too, heard the sound, and John realized that all her feelings had been mixed up in the last month, for now she was crying and shivering and leaning weakly on Lillian simply because her brother was dead. All social thoughts that might have embittered her from the manner of his death were absolutely unimportant now, and John, liking her more at the moment, when there was not bitterness in it for her and just the natural sorrow, than he had liked her at any time the last three months, moved closer, wanting to put his arm around her and be one with her in her affection and her sorrow. But he did not touch her at all. Even at that moment, looking at Lillian, he knew he could not touch Isabelle, whom he had loved in the old days, in front of her without feeling embarrassed.

The wide-hipped aunt, enormous in an overcoat, took hold of Isabelle's hand, patting and rubbing it as though expecting the girl to faint. Isabelle withdrew her hand abruptly. "Please, don't," she said. All her social feelings were restored when the aunt touched her, knowing how she felt about Fred. The big woman was annoyed because Isabelle, starting to cry, was simply behaving properly, and deserving to be comforted.

"Now, Isabelle," the aunt said.

"Please, Mrs. Harcourt, don't touch me."

The aunt looked at John and Ed Henley, shaking her head and closing her eyes several times.

Walking up from the slope to the automobiles at the cemetery gate, Isabelle said to John: "You won't mind if Lillian comes home and has dinner with us, John?"

"Not at all."

"Will you come over afterward?"

"At any time. About eight o'clock."

"Would you like to come home, too?"

"No, I'd rather not, Isabelle. I'll come later."

On the way back to the city John and the two neighbors and Ed Henley were in the cab. The nervous one no longer found it necessary to look at his watch, and seemed quite satisfied and happy again. The tall man smiled, showing all the long, white teeth, and said: "Well, that's done."

"We did all we could, anyway," the short one said.

"We simply had to do it." They went on talking about the bad time Isabelle and her mother would have, living in the city.

Ed Henley tried to interest John in stories about Fred, talking rather awkwardly, uncertain whether he was being appreciated. His winged collar had begun to bother him and he kept putting a forefinger down between his neck and the collar buttons.

"I'm not much used to these collars," he said apologetically.

"They are a bother," John said.

"Just the same I think I'll go down to St. Agnes Club with it on tonight and give the boys a treat."

"What club is that?"

"It's a boxing club. I work out there a couple of times a week. You ought to come out."

"Oh, you're a fighter, eh?"

"Just an amateur, but I'm going in the city tournaments next month. That's where I met Fred, out at the club. He wasn't half bad with the gloves." The man's hands did not bother him now and he went on talking about his weight the rest of the way down the street, asking each one of the neighbors what he weighed and offering to guess John's weight. "The only thing the matter with me is that my legs are built like a light heavyweight and I'm only tall enough for the middleweight," he said. The two neighbors became very interested in him and felt the muscles on his arms.

John, turning up his coat collar, got out of the cab at Bloor Street, in the uptown section of the city, in the drizzling rain. It was not quite noontime, and in the armchair lunch, having a cup of coffee, he decided not to go to work in the afternoon. Sipping hot coffee out of the thick, white mug he carried on, in his own mind, the conversation with Ed Henley, suddenly angry that Isabelle should have any kind of intimacy with such a fellow. First he was calmly curious about the nature of such an intimacy, then resentfully angry to think of it at all.

CHAPTER FOUR

O n the way over to the Thompson house, walking briskly, his head was down and both hands were in his pockets. It was bothering him that Lillian should have gone home with Isabelle, so eager to go on sharing all her feelings, and worrying him because he was in love with Lillian and all the last few months they had had few good times together because they always had to go on thinking of these other people when they ought to be having intensely happy moments. Such thoughts as these were not all at once in his head as he walked east, swinging his left leg so the toe turned in, but it became a strong feeling inside him, passing an automobile parked at the curb and seeing a fellow and a girl huddled together in the back seat, their arms around each other. It was not even dark, just a steady twilight, and lights were not lit on the street. Sidewalks had dried after the noon rain but the trunks and branches of trees, almost stripped of leaves now, were darkly damp, the bark holding the moisture. Ashamed of such thoughts about Lillian and Isabelle, he smiled, for it was only natural that Lillian should be glad to be in the company of Isabelle when it was an unhappy time for her, but even walking a little faster he couldn't get rid of the steady, strong feeling. Twice he was ready to speak angrily to Isabelle as soon as he saw her but each time was ashamed of the notion.

He went into the house without knocking because he was such an old friend of the Thompsons. Lillian and Isabelle were walking together on the back veranda, their voices coming to him, and he tapped on the window.

When they were sitting down together Isabelle said: "We were just talking about you."

"I was thinking of both of you coming along the street."

"Mother is lying down. I don't know whether or not she's sleeping."

"Is she feeling all right?"

"I haven't known for a long time how she has felt about it all."

Lillian had told Isabelle that John was leaving the department store to devote all his time to singing.

"I daresay you didn't like the notion of working in the store," Isabelle said suddenly.

"That's it."

"It's beneath you."

"Not exactly."

"That's it. It is beneath you. A man ought to get away from the things that are beneath him."

Lillian said casually: "I'm glad he's quitting there. I want him to, as long as he can get along without it."

"Then you both simply feel the same way."

Isabelle asked Lillian to go in and see if Mrs. Thompson was resting. John and Isabelle sat alone on the back porch beside each other in the rocking chairs, hardly moving, watching lights come on in the back windows of houses on the other side of the block. The lights shone palely in the windows because it was hardly dark. The air was warmer than it had been in the afternoon, a warm, light breeze blowing from the east.

"Practically all the flowers are gone now," Isabelle said.

Stems of flowers were still standing in the garden earth: withered flowers with broken stems; a few asters and zinnias still in bloom but fading in the daytime sun; tall stalks of flowers lying dry and dead against the fence. The leaves were still thick on the grapevine.

"I hate to see the last of them go," she said. "I worked with them all summer."

"They were very beautiful in the warm summer months."

Watching her carefully, waiting for her to say something that would arouse him sooner or later, he began to rock rapidly, steadily, in the chair, catching a glimpse of the side of her face at the same angle every time. Since she had become so much thinner her nose now was almost too large for her face, and her forehead and chin were too prominent. Wetting her lips, she continued looking toward the garden, her bright eyes hardly wavering, because she was not thinking of the garden. She had on a black crepe dress, a collar high on her neck. The dress was a little too large, there was not movement under it, the cloth folds were unnaturally still.

"You ought to take care of yourself from now on," he said rather formally.

"I suppose so. I'm not much to look at now."

"You'll soon be looking lovely again."

"Now that we've started talking, what do you think I ought to do from now on?"

"What do you mean?"

"I mean how am I going to live? Who am I going to love? Who am I going to be happy with?"

"You oughtn't to go on looking at it in that way, Isabelle."

"Of course not, John. But I can't have many friends."

"You can. You have."

"You and Lillian, but who else now?"

She spoke casually and coolly, hurting herself with her own words and hurting John, too, who glared at her suddenly, uttering words she could not hear. He wanted to shake her for her silly determination to hurt him with the words about her brother.

"Look here," he said impulsively, "I was fond of Fred, too. Stop talking about it. What is there to be gained by having all our old thoughts again? Why do you have to torture yourself and hurt me, too? I won't have it, do you hear, Isabelle? I'll not have another word of it. I won't sit here if you go on talking about it. I'll go around the alleyway there and not come back for a long time."

"Sit down, John."

"I'm sorry, Isabelle. I ought not to talk like that to you tonight."

"I know, John. It's got into your mind something like the way it's got into mine."

"Only differently."

"Yes. But I was simply asking you what I ought to do."

"Find some kind of work. Something to take up your time."

"When I quit work in the office I knew I could never go back and have the people staring at me. Where else could I go where the same thing wouldn't happen? I suppose I ought to get married."

"It would be better for everybody."

"But who around here even likes to have us for neighbors now? They point at the house when they pass. They're sorry for Mother and me and would no doubt do things for us. The men around here, who've looked at me, look at me as though I ought to be an easy mark from now on. That's why I didn't think you and I ought to get married."

"Maybe we wouldn't have, anyway."

"Maybe we wouldn't. But you see what your feeling would have been if we had gone on? We would have had the same feeling and have had to stay on the outside of things."

"Listen, Isabelle, you have your friends. You know Lillian and I both are with you. I love Lillian and we'll get married and that'll help you, too."

"You'll get married soon?"

"We can't get married for a couple of years, because I want to go away and have my voice trained."

"That will be lovely, but you shouldn't bother with me if you want to get on in this city. People will hold it against you."

"Nonsense. Stop talking about it."

"But whom do you think I ought to marry?"

"Please let's not talk about it at all."

"You will do very well with your singing. The best churches in the city will have you as soloist and for concert work. Lillian will be your accompanist. Won't it be lovely?"

"I hope so."

"Lillian is rather sweet, but if she begins to get on at all, she'll resent it if people talk to her about me."

"You should be having some good thoughts about Lillian."

"I do. At nighttime when often I couldn't go to sleep and felt I had to think of something beautiful I thought of the way it was with you and Lillian."

He said angrily: "Sit here if you want to, I'm going in." Though he got up quickly she held his arm, and when he tugged twice, held it tightly, so he sat down slowly. "I'm not trying to be nasty," she said quietly, her mouth remaining open a little, as though she were puzzled by her own thoughts. Refusing to look directly at her at all, he rocked vigorously in the chair.

"The trouble with you is that you think you have to be hard about it," he said.

"I know."

"You don't have to be hard about it."

"I'm not trying to be hard."

"In your own thoughts you are keeping too much in the shadows. It's over now, I tell you . . . ."

"It's never over."

"It's over now, and you in your own thoughts are dodging in and out of the shadowy places and all the time it keeps getting darker in your own heart. And soon there's no relief. Isabelle, dear Isabelle, let the hours and the days go slowly and easily. Sometimes I can feel you jeering at me and rebuffing me, just out of your own hardness. Do you remember when I used to say you were so sweetly soft in your own nature you were far too kind to other people? My God, soon you must start smiling and then laugh out loud."

"Give me time. I will."

"It's too soon now, yes, but you must, I tell you."

"But it's so hard to laugh out loud when someone hearing you might be startled, then indignant. If only I could have it as it was a year ago. If I could just have all over again for a little while, the same friends and the same pleasures and never grow any older. But I have you. I must never let you go."

"No need of it, dear."

She seemed suddenly feverish, for her shoulders were trembling, though she was holding herself tightly, and he wished she would suddenly start to cry. There was nothing for him to say. His chair rocked steadily on the veranda. It was dark now in the garden and he could hardly see the stems of the few flowers, and sniffing eagerly he caught faintly the scent of the rose bush with the three small blooms. His feeling of resentment was becoming stronger, as he moved restlessly, now definitely angry with Isabelle, and ready to shake her if she held on to him with her words again. He said suddenly:

"The three roses are rather late, aren't they?"

"Every year they come just at about this time."

"I can just faintly get the odor."

"They haven't much odor at this time of year."

"Are you thinking of cutting them?"

"No, we leave them on the bush every year till the petals fall."

It was suddenly lighter than it had been before, thick clouds had opened and a strong clear moon shone in a dark sky, the moon riding in the dark blotch and the light clouds all around it. The moonlight shone on the garage roofs in yards, glinting on tin roofs and shining on the brick chimneys and throwing the long shadow on the houses. On the brick wall of the house three doors away were mauve shades and light tans and a small peach tree in the backyard had its branches outlined on this wall.

"Ed Henley is coming around. He ought to be here soon," she said.

"Why do you have him around, Isabelle?"

"Don't you like him?"

"He's all right. He's cheap, that's all."

"He likes me."

"Oh, well."

"And he knew Fred."

"I know."

"The point is I think I fascinate him now. I met him a year or so ago and he seemed almost afraid of me, and now he's not a bit afraid and at the same time I fascinate him."

"What does he hope for?"

"I don't know. He knows I'm apt to be an easy mark from now on, and anyway he's a bit proud of knowing me."

"I don't like him at all. He's too ridiculous."

"Maybe, but I'm glad to have someone like that around now."

They heard the front door open. "That's probably Ed now," she said, without getting up. "Lillian can talk to him."

So they sat silently in the chair, and John, listening intently for every small sound from the house, heard Lillian speaking to Ed and imagined them sitting down together in the front room while she talked sympathetically with him, liking him simply because he was Isabelle's friend. Leaning forward, he listened but could hear hardly a word; then there were no sounds at all. He heard Lillian laughing faintly and got up quickly.

"I'm going in the house," he said.

"You're not jealous of Ed, surely."

Enraged, he did not answer, merely turning, going into the house. Isabelle followed him. In the room at the front of the house Lillian and Ed Henley were sitting together trying awkwardly to make pleasant conversation. John, hardly shaking hands with Henley, said to Lillian, "I was thinking we might go along now."

"Do you remember we were talking about the tournament this afternoon, Mr. Hughes?" Henley said cheerfully.

"I remember."

"I'm working out tomorrow night, would you like to come over?"

"I don't care to, thanks," John said rudely.

"All right, as long as you're not being snooty."

"He's not really snooty," Isabelle said quickly. "Only in some ways he's a little beyond us. Aren't you, John?"

"Don't be silly, Isabelle. Lillian and I are going. Are you staying here?"

Isabelle said she wanted Ed to walk over to the church with her so she could say a few prayers.

On the street with Lillian he said: "I thought if we hurried we might get downtown in time to see a show."

"I don't feel much like a show tonight."

"There's absolutely no reason why we shouldn't see a show tonight, unless we're too late."

So they walked through the side streets downtown, and before they got to the car tracks they could see the tall white towers of the Sterling building with the lights in angles at the top shining on the ornamental green stone.

They were too late to get into a vaudeville show. They went to a restaurant, afterward walking slowly, looking into the brightly lighted store windows. They had no unpleasant conversation, and John was happier than he had been all week, because they were only talking about simple thoughts not at all complicated and were glad to be alone together. He liked Lillian's slim neck and the curling ends of hair under her hat on her neck. Then they talked earnestly about the good times they were going to have in a few years after he had returned from Europe and was being praised by all the critics in all the big cities, taking it for granted he would have enough money to go away, and they would go on thinking about each other and get married as soon as he returned. They were walking now in the quiet streets by the dark warehouses and agreeing he ought to give a recital as soon as possible and invite all the prominent people.

CHAPTER FIVE

*F*or a week he was satisfied with the way he was letting the days go by. In the morning he lay in bed till noon, lazily letting the sunlight from the windows on the north side of the house fall over him, stretched out on the bed. Then he got up and sat by the window, his nose pressed against the glass, looking down into the street. Three or four kids were playing on the lawns. Watching the kids playing was a simple pleasure, because he knew them by sight and had heard their voices at the same time every morning. Watching lazily at the window he had got to know the relation of the kids: the little bully, the one who lived next door, cried easily; two or three simply followed the others, always a little behind when they ran across the street. Mrs. Errington, plump and round-faced wearing a heather-colored sweater-coat, was raking leaves off the front grass and talking at the same time to the woman next door, who was poking with a stick at a flower rockery in a corner formed by the front step and the width of her veranda. A vegetable man, his wagon across the road heaped with fresh market produce, called across the street to Mrs. Errington and held up three cobs of fresh corn. The street was all a small, simple, orderly world and John Hughes sat for almost an hour at the window, listening alertly, and smiling to himself whenever he was amused. He wanted it always to be the same. Mrs. Errington, looking up at the window, waved to him and he nodded to her.

The good, simple, joyful feeling remained with him in the bathroom, shaving, and he sang in his strong voice all the vowel sounds in a scale, between each stroke of the razor looking at himself steadily in the mirror, going up the scale, holding the last note a long time. Fully dressed, he went downstairs to the front room, and standing by the piano, touching the keys with only one finger, practiced the scales for an hour longer. No one was in the house; everything was the way he wanted it to be.

In the late afternoon he played tennis with Lillian on the private court in the north end of the city, a cinder court with a red fence between it and the railway embankment. When a train passed and the smoke drifted over the court it was hard to see the ball. John played energetically till he was all tired out, then sat in the shade on the clubhouse bench earnestly watching Lillian, who was playing lazily with some other girl, noting the shape of her head, and the childishly happy expression on her face when she won a game, noting it carefully as though she were a stranger and he was admiring her for the first time.

In the evening he took his singing lesson from Hobson, remaining with him and his wife for several hours, listening to the old man's stories about the days when oratorio singers were celebrated in England and the good times he had had at the Savage Club. He wanted John to go to England in a few years and do oratorio work. Since he had never done much himself in opera, he had no use for teachers of it, and advised all his pupils to study for oratorio. But his wife was always encouraging, and they had tea and small cakes, the three of them talking excitedly, gossiping, and disparaging all other singers in the city and their instructors till it was time for John to leave and walk home.

But he had avoided Isabelle all week, and when Lillian talked about her he shrugged his shoulders, hardly interested. The night they were at the theater, seeing Janet Cowl in *Romeo and Juliet*, she said between the first and second act:

"Isabelle and I were talking about you last night."

"What's that?"

"Isabelle and I were talking together and she talked about you."

"Yeah," he said, hardly touched by the feeling that so often excited him.

"She's upset and excitable, but when we're together I like her more than I ever liked a woman."

"It's good you are together," he said.

And then he shook his head at Lillian, laughing a little foolishly as though he had acted last week like a simple-minded man and now was feeling sure of himself again. By expressing this opinion of his feeling and having Lillian understand, it was easier to keep the notion that he had behaved badly last week, but it was over now; and then expressing the pleasure of his own thoughts from the beauty of the play and the actress, he said: "Let's go canoeing together on Saturday night out at the bluffs."

At the end of the week, early in the evening, they went canoeing out east near the dance hall by The Hundred Steps, a little way along from the bluffs. It was the last night the dance hall would be open and there would be hardly any canoeing after the weekend because the lake water was cold and the nights were too cool in October. They were both expecting a happier, finer evening together than they had had all week, and John had been very contented and peaceful in the mornings in his room by the window, when all the thoughts he attached to a picture of her in his mind were happy and concerned with her alone, and he had looked forward to having on this evening at the lake with her a high point in a strong common feeling.

At early twilight they were at The Hundred Steps and the afternoon crowd from the beach was going home. The Steps, beyond the city limits, ran down from the height of land and a street of good houses to the natural beach below. They hired a canoe at the boathouse under the dance hall and John began to paddle toward the bluffs, paddling easily and slowly, hardly glancing ahead, looking directly at Lillian, her body comfortable in the cushions. Occasionally he looked at the blue water still sparkling on the wave-crests in the sunlight. Lillian was so cool and fair and slender and smiling he could hardly go on paddling, and though her eyes were half closed she was sensitive to all his thoughts and her fingers began to move nervously over her throat and two faint red spots were on her cheeks. Lillian's sensitivity had nothing to do with a feeling of embarrassment between them: it was a feeling that had been getting stronger, and whenever it was in one and they were alone it was quickly in the other. Usually the feeling was first in John, then she began to feel all the force of it inside her and they didn't know what to do. It was not possible for them to get married, because all the money John had saved was to be for his musical education in another country and she was happier believing it ought to be that way.

"You are lovely," he said suddenly.

"Am I?"

"You're lovely and I want to do something about it."

"Keep on paddling."

"No, I want to let the paddle trail in the water and try to make it clear how lovely you are."

"But what is there to do? I'm lovely and that's settled, and it's very beautiful here on the water."

"Live with me and love me."

"It can't be done, dear one."

"Let's do something right now. I'll turn in toward the shore."

"No, we'll not do it."

"We'll go up and sit on that little hill over there by the two tall trees."

"No, you're not going to get me over there."

"Well, here then."

"No, you'll muss me, and sit still, for heaven's sake."

"We ought to be living together," he said.

"We ought to and perhaps I'm foolish, but I wouldn't feel right about it unless we were married."

"You love me enough for it."

"Yes. But you've been at me so long."

He held the paddle loosely, letting it float on the surface of the water. His hand was in the cold water up to his wrist. The water felt very clean and cold on his wrist. The canoe was drifting in toward the bluffs. All the way along from the dance hall the hills had been getting high and steeper till they became tall pinnacled clay crags high over the water's edge, with just enough beach for a path across the base. No sand was on the narrow beach at the base of the tallest bluffs; just smooth pebbles piled thickly, some of them dry and white. She said suddenly, casually: "We both should be feeling sorry for Isabelle now."

"But why now?"

"It's lovely here on the water in the twilight."

"It's lovely here on the water, but what of it."

"Well, she was in love with you."

"I was in love with her."

"Now she's being just a bit too hectic with Ed Henley."

"Is he her lover?"

"I think so. I think he has slept with her."

"Good God, what a bedfellow."

"But he expected to, don't you think? And he's very nice to her. I'm terribly sorry and never think of it as touching her at all. I don't think she's well. She's jaunty now, but she's in bad health."

The careless happiness, drifting on the still water, was almost gone and several times he muttered to himself, looking eagerly at Lillian and soberly dragging the tip of one finger in the water, trying to hold on to the former feeling of the other moment. They were both anxious for the feeling they were losing, and shaking her head stubbornly she said: "Sing very quietly, just a little song, John." He began to sing softly a song made from a poem of A.E. Housman's called "Summer Time on Bredon," singing quietly, though his voice carried far over the water. It was getting dark and they could hardly see other boats near them, but heard voices and laughter coming over the water, and he stopped singing the song which was not making them feel any better and said sharply: "Lillian, listen to me. Do you think I'm still in love with Isabelle?"

"I don't know."

"I tell you definitely I'm not."

"We both love her."

"Why can't you see that I don't? Why do you have to be so calm about it?" He was pounding the side of the canoe with his fist, his head leaning forward, his mouth hanging open.

"You didn't have to mention it at all, you know," she said.

"Maybe not. Why do they call the bluffs over there 'The Dutch Cathedral'?"

"Look at them with your eyes half closed and they look like cathedral spires."

He was paddling toward the dance hall, the rows of colored lights shining now on the terrace, and shining on the water. All the way back, hardly speaking, they were in the clear path of the moonlit water, but behind the water was dark and ahead, out beyond the dance hall, it shimmered iridescently. John, a little ashamed of his own sudden anger, was paddling skillfully. Lillian, lying back in the canoe, hardly looked at him, sincerely interested in her own thoughts.

"What are you thinking of?" he said casually, to help make a friendly conversation.

"Fred Thompson."

"Fred Thompson?"

"Yes."

"Why?"

"I don't know. Thoughts of him just came into my head when you asked me about Isabelle. I don't know if I used to love Fred."

"Eh? What's that?"

"I hardly had time to love Fred, I suppose."

"You didn't know him hardly. You knew him about a month."

"I know. I was very fond of him. Maybe I was in love with him."

"That's nonsense, do you hear, you've got that thought in your head now. I don't know why it should come into your head, do you hear? Fred Thompson is dead. He's very, very dead."

"I just like to think about him."

"But he's dead and you hardly knew him. You've got to believe that." The boat was rocking jerkily as he leaned forward, trying to get on his knees. Wagging the finger of his right hand at her, he fumbled for words, wetting his lower lip rapidly with his tongue. The light was on one side of his face.

"I tell you something and you become absurd," she said angrily.

"Maybe I am. I know it. I can't help it."

"I'm sorry, John."

"Dear Lillian." Still he was speaking huskily and paddling nervously, frowning, trying hard to understand his own feeling. They heard music from the dance hall coming over the water and saw fellows and girls going down the pavilion steps, strolling along the beach to get in the shadows of the trees on the hill.

"Do you want to dance?" he said.

"We'll dance twice and go home."

So they beached the canoe and paid, and danced in the small pavilion, but found it hard to make interesting conversation. They left the dance hall and climbed up The Hundred Steps, walking carefully where the railing had fallen away, to the lighted street on the hill. His shoulders were hunched forward as he pulled the joints on his fingers, making the cracking noises.

"Please don't make those noises," she said.

"I'm sorry, Lillian. You believe I'm sorry, don't you?"

It had been fine and still and peaceful on the water by the cliffs. Far out on the lake there were paths of light on the dark water.

Chapter Six

---

*C*oming out of Massey Hall late in the evening after hearing Sophie Braslau sing, they were slowly walking the short block to the corner, still holding some of the agreeable feeling they had experienced listening to the contralto. On one side of the street in the short block were old houses with narrow lawns. In the damp ground and mud on the lawn a line of fresh footprints was firmly marked. In the light from the street lamp edges of the footprints were firmly outlined and hardening in the wind.

"I've been thinking of something nearly all evening," she said.

"Tell me."

"You remember the other evening asking me to love you, live with you?"

"Yes."

"I've been thinking I could get a small apartment if you'd pay just a little bit a month toward it."

"You've been thinking that?"

"That's what I'm thinking."

"You mean we might live together?"

"No, but we could have the place and you could come when you wanted."

"Oh, how absolutely wonderful."

His joy was simple and honest and he had hardly any words to express it because of the directness of her acceptance of something that had been beyond his persuasion. He held on to her arm, walking along the street, and when she trembled a little he had his own aching sensation. It was not easy for her to give herself to him because her family had been religiously sober and most of her own emotions were always restrained and expressed conventionally, and even though he did not think of that part of it at all, it was there to increase the intensity of his feeling. At this time she was living with an aunt in the west end of the city, a maiden lady who owned a good deal of property, and who had a big brick house with a wide veranda overlooking High Park. Usually he went into the house in the evening with Lillian and talked to the aunt while she made a cup of tea for them, but tonight they stood on the veranda, holding each other tightly and there seemed to be no strength in her body. It was all soft, as though she had been hanging on to herself a long time and had got suddenly tired. There was a couch on one end of the veranda, and lifting her up suddenly he tried to lie down with her on the couch.

"No, we can't now," she said. "It wouldn't be safe for me."

"We ought to now."

"It would be bad for me that way," she said. Her face was white and her eyes moist, but she held on to this one practical thought. So laughing, he kissed her, and laughed at himself, mussing her hair. Though it was cool, a damp breeze blowing over the big pond in the lowland in the park, he would not go into the house because he didn't want to see or speak to anyone else.

"You've thought it all over?" he said, still feeling she should agree with him only after some kind of a stubborn pressure.

"Well, it's what you want, isn't it?"

"Yes, but I want you to be happy, too."

"It had to happen some time. You've been at me all summer and we might as well do it decently and then I'll be happier having my own place."

Going home he walked several blocks before it occurred to him to get a streetcar. On the car he was sure his face was solemnly expressionless and sat down hurriedly, smiling a little, and trying to get a sullen expression on his face. An elderly woman holding a sleeping child in her arms smiled at him: the woman, thinking he was smiling at the expression on the child's face, pulled back the blanket from one eye and smiled again and John glared at her.

Hardly looking at him the woman said: "Do you like babies, mister?"

"Sometimes, madam." Ashamed of his curtness, he added quickly, "It's a lovely child. How old is it?"

"Three months. He looks nice now, but you should see him in the daytime. His expression is altogether different."

The woman, red-faced and cheerful, spoke with a broad accent, and he was obliged to hold this conversation with her till she got off the car, then ridiculing her to himself, a vulgar woman, he tried hard to get again the flow of the fine thoughts of Lillian.

At home he went to bed and did not bother to read. He turned out the light and lay awake in the bed and heard faintly the Erringtons talking in their bedroom. On the front veranda, underneath his bedroom, two cats were moaning softly. The Erringtons' cat, a Maltese, sat on a cushion in the chair that was on the veranda every night and the two cats came to see it later in the evening. They kept on moaning at each other till the electrician, who lived next door, opened his bedroom window and made strange hissing noises, and they ran away into an alley further down the street.

All week he was tender and patient and considerate of Lillian, just as though they were going to be married, and on Saturday night she took him to see the apartment on the third floor in a new apartment house in the north end of the city, and the window looked out on a wide lawn and hedges. The building was only two minutes' walk from the corner and the car line, and, the other way, only ten minutes to the end of the street and down the path to the ravine. They were a little shy, standing together alone for the first time in the room this afternoon, while she told him she had decided to give lessons on the piano, and it might, in a few months, be even more economical to have the apartment. He was hardly listening, knowing that in a few moments he would be making love to her and she was just talking herself into the mood for it. They were looking out the window at the hedges. It was a new street and a vacant lot with trees was between the apartment house and the next house. The hedges were turning brown, and two small birds were darting at them, rising and darting farther along. A little sunlight glinted on the humming birds' small bodies, brilliant-breasted, as they pivoted in the air, almost hovering in one spot, tumbling and darting into the hedge again. The air was still and quiet in the afternoon sunlight and the small wings whirred but could hardly be seen: then they were out of sight, but the wings whirred farther along the hedge, and they balanced and ducked and the sunlight glinted again.

"How beautiful," she said.

But she cried a little, sitting down when he started to make love to her, and wanted him to do everything slowly.

It was all new to her and she kept both fists shut tightly at first, closing her eyes as though determined to shut out her own feeling, giving herself to him for the first time. She was a small slim woman and her eyes were shut, her mouth open a little, all her muscles relaxed, and she was almost too fragile. This physical fragility and weakness was apparent only when she was without tension, with her eyes closed.

He stayed with her all that first night.

After practicing with the choir at the church, or the nights he was free, he came to the apartment, and they were happy with amusements, which seemed suddenly to become more important than anything else in life. The most difficult songs he practiced with her at the piano, and they were happy because their attention was taken into their work, till his voice tired and he began to clear his throat noisily, his lips closed, looking serious and dignified, and walking to the far corner of the room. Lillian kept on playing the piano while he sat down watching her; so happily aware of her perfection for him the music lost all design. She was playing the piano, glancing at him occasionally over her shoulder, then seriously regarding the sheet of music. Lillian enjoyed music because it always gave her fresh experience and meant, to her personally, something beyond the melody or the rhythm that was in the piece. She was at the piano long after he was tired, still getting the full value and suggestion of the notes. Her ear was better than his, never tiring so quickly, and she retained a sense of personal experience after he heard objectively only the sounds.

They had cakes and tea and sandwiches while talking eagerly about his voice. The ambition between them was for his voice and how it might develop later on with careful training. They agreed it was getting a little fuller and becoming absolutely effortless. Later they had a small brandy and he shook his head seriously, asking for another one. The brandy warmed them and they did not talk so earnestly about the singing and the music, and she wanted to be petted and loved gently till it was no longer necessary to talk at all. For the rest of the evening she was almost religiously obedient to all his wishes, as though it were a new excitement and a pleasure to do anything he suggested.

They had the brandy at the same time almost every evening.

After he had made love to her he went home, for they did not want the caretaker in the apartment house to think she was a loose woman. He liked going home to the room in the Erringtons' house; he could lie awake and think of loving Lillian. The walk home was over the viaduct, and he was always glad when he came along the street and looked up at the house and saw the windows of his room over the veranda. The Maltese cat curled up on the cushion on the veranda chair was not disturbed, for he came home at this time every night.

On Sunday evening Isabelle was with Lillian when he came to the apartment. She would not wear mourning and had on a red felt hat. Her lips were red and she was sitting carelessly on the arm of a chair, talking enthusiastically.

"Dear John," she said.

"It's fine to have you here, Isabelle."

"If I had only known how nice it was I would have been here before."

He was almost shy with Lillian and embarrassed, looking at Isabelle, for he did not know her feeling. Lillian and Isabelle went on talking rapidly as if they had many important things to discuss in a hurry. Isabelle was too cheerful, too determinedly good-natured. They were talking about a scandal that had been in the papers, and then Isabelle got up, walking around the room, looking at the furniture and the bed, the rugs on the floor and then at the bed again. The furniture, though not expensive, interested her, and she nodded her head, expressing appreciation of everything as she crossed the room quickly, her body bent forward a little and stood at the window. Twice she turned, glancing at John, who was sitting uncomfortably a few feet away from her, and looking at him, she smiled, merely trying to indicate that in her own way she was sharing their good time and it was not necessary to talk about it at all. Before sitting down she suddenly put her arms around John and kissed him. Her lips were firm, hardly moving when she kissed him and said, "I love both of you."

"Are you feeling any better?" John said.

"I get a little feverish easily, but I do think it makes me look a little livelier. Could we have a drink now?"

"I'm getting a little brandy for the three of us," Lillian said.

John said, "Are you doing anything at all these days, Isabelle?"

"Not a thing, John; just loafing."

Amused, she glanced at him and he smiled, holding the one expression on his face till Lillian returned with the brandy. Isabelle drank very quickly and said lazily: "I suppose you're around here a lot now, John?"

"Early in the evenings mainly."

"Lillian's lovely isn't she?"

"Very."

"You know I'll be feeling good for days thinking of you here with Lillian. It's almost better than letting Ed Henley marry me. He wants to marry me. Can you imagine a man like that?"

"You love him," he said resentfully.

"I like him and he's comforting. Why do you resent any affection I have for that fellow?"

"I don't, but you can't marry him. Promise me you won't marry him," he said, reaching out, holding her hand and squeezing it. Lillian, who had been staring at Isabelle started biting her lip, trying to keep from crying, because she felt that everything was prepared for the beginning of her own happiness and Isabelle was too intent upon degrading herself. Isabelle, insisting she might marry Ed Henley, shook her head stubbornly as if compelled to go on with a plan that was necessary, though disagreeable. Wrinkling the corners of her eyes she stared at the floor, then said brightly: "John, tell me, when will Paul Ross be coming back to town?"

"Within a week or two. Why?"

"Will you ask him to phone me?"

"You really don't know him well."

"Oh, you fix it."

"All right, I'll fix it."

"You'll fix it, will you?"

"Absolutely."

"Then I'll go along now. I've got a date. So long."

After she had gone there was no easy flow of conversation because John couldn't find ready words, sitting alone, wondering why he could not standing thinking of Isabelle marrying Ed Henley.

Lillian, standing by the window, swung aside the curtains. "Isabelle's worrying you, John, dear," she said.

"Nonsense, how can such a pretty girl be so ridiculous."

"It's not ridiculous; it's just that Isabelle's worrying you."

"Wrong, my love."

"You were sitting there thinking of her."

"Wrong again," he smiled.

"The grin on your face is hideous, it's so false."

"All right, I'll look solemn and sullen."

"Don't bother. Tell me, instead, how far did your affair with Isabelle go? I mean did you actually love her? Isn't that the way to put it? I mean was everything easy between you so you could touch her when you felt like it?"

"I never touched her, Lillian."

"Honestly?"

"Honest to God."

"You did, by the way you say it."

"I touch wood. I didn't"

"Did you used to have quaint amusing expressions and an intimate ritual just the two of you shared?"

"I tell you we never went in for that at all. Occasionally we kissed, that's all. But, Lord, let up, Lillian, it's too much like a coroner's inquest at the morgue."

"Were they lovely long kisses, sweetheart?"

"Shut up, Lillian. Come away from that window. What's the matter with you tonight?"

"I'll tell you explicitly, shall I?"

"Please do."

"Well, you were so obviously uneasy when Isabelle was in the room I felt like your second wife acting hostess to your first wife who has just called, particularly when she glanced in the bedroom and you looked as if you had been caught playing hookey from school. I'd feel happier in this apartment if you'd swear you didn't know what girls and Isabelle were all about, and you were just Lillian's little white-headed boy."

"I'll take a pledge. Come here and sit down. In reality I'm a Y.M.C.A. secretary."

"You come over here by the window."

"Here I am then, now what?"

"See how clear the night air is out over the city and the houses, and the hill and the lights slope downtown, and the pink and yellow lights on the high signboards are reflected so brilliantly there seem to be no stars in the sky."

"Our city, I suppose. Sometimes it's bright and sometimes it's shoddy but . . ."

"A bright and shoddy city where John, the troubadour, was often discouraged because the Conservatory of Music had a monopoly in the city."

"A bright city where Lillian lost her heart but not her head to a sullen young singer."

"A shoddy city where Lillian lost her virginity to the same sullen fellow."

"A bright city, where the sullen young man and the hapless virgin, now despoiled, stood at the window looking out over the city and finally kissed each other."

"But don't bite me, please," she said.

They talked about Isabelle again on Saturday afternoon after they had walked east on the apartment house street and had gone down the ravine, finally walking along the old belt line, an abandoned railroad track through the valley. This afternoon Lillian was trying to conceal that she was uneasy from thinking of loving him so freely with a marriage so far away. Since he had expected her to have sometimes such a feeling he did not trouble her with questions, and she did not irritate him by talking, knowing the unhappiness was only temporary, because she hadn't got used to the new way of living. She felt she was really happier, but still close to an old way of thinking. The rusty track was on a high ridge in a narrow valley and the ties, sunk in the ground, were almost covered by earth and grass. The valley slopes were thickly wooded and alongside the track ridge a small stream ran noisily over worn flat rocks. It was the middle of October and leaves that had not fallen were red and brown, and on the hill trees were patches of green and blotches of brown, and beautiful red leaves. October was often a fine month, but when red and brown leaves fell slowly it was the last of the fine months and it was easy to enjoy thoughts pleasantly sad, feeling in the one mood with the hills and bare trees. Lillian, walking along the track slowly, a long twig in her hand she used to poke at the ties, was having an uneasy feeling from a lack of security, thinking of her family in the country and the values she had always thought important. It was much easier, being already in the mood, to take a pleasure in a groping for remembrances to strengthen her emotion, and she remembered one of the few walks she had ever taken with Fred Thompson along this old belt line, only it had been in the spring on a first warm day, and she had tripped and fallen over one of the ties.

"It was in the early spring," she said, "and Fred was carrying a light coat and we sat down back there by the bridge."

"He had an absurd theory just about that time," John said, "that it was important he should enjoy himself completely." Fred had gone to the war and it had taken four years, and afterward his first concern had become the complete enjoyment of himself. They talked about Fred Thompson, each adding a memory, a brief picture of him, fragmentary recollections, giving him life, as they walked along the track. Fred had laughed at John's notion that he might be an artist singing the compositions of other men, and had thought it of no more importance than bricklaying or snow shoveling. One day he had taken John aside to ask him if he thought it worthwhile studying hard for so many years, thinking always of an elusive fame, when he might begin at once to have a good time by simply considering himself as an unimportant part of the life around him. The war years had given Fred the feeling that an individual was hardly of any importance at all, and at first his notions had become anarchistic; then, loafing in the daytime, he had started reading about the Middle Ages and thought it a beautiful time when all the people and scholars were part of a cultural plan giving shape to the life around them. He liked to think it might someday be that way in his own country, but was too lazy to do anything but lie on the grass, his long legs crossed at the ankles, and talk enthusiastically with his eyes closed. He had got hold of a pleasant idea and liked talking about it.

John began to speak eagerly to Lillian of days when Fred and he were kids and they had come up into the hills after school, only they had called it the "bush" then because it made it seem farther away, though really only part of the park valley beyond the city limits. They were having this conversation all along the narrow ravine till it widened out into the main valley and they saw, far across, all the houses on one side and down below, the tall dark chimneys of the brickyards, and down the valley, over the Don River, the big white viaduct with the red cars moving.

Suddenly John said: "Look here, Lillian, why did you move into the apartment if it bothers you and makes you unhappy."

"Because I thought it would be best for both of us, but now I can't seem to get used to it. I keep thinking we ought to be married."

"I mean what really put the thought into your head?"

"I told Isabelle about the way we were feeling and we talked a little."

"She thought it would be better for you to get an apartment?"

"She thought it might be better to be practical and in the long run it would be better for both of us."

"Isabelle really persuaded you."

"She helped me think and make up my mind."

"I say she persuaded you. Do you hear?"

He would not talk any more, staring down at one of the rusty tracks. He did not want to look up at her, simply following the line of the track. Earnestly he was concentrating on the surface of the track. "So, that's it, is it?" he muttered once. "That's it. That's it. She's got a hold of you." Lillian held on to his arm but he would not talk at all.

CHAPTER SEVEN

*T*wice before the end of the month, John sang out of town, short trips with small payment and Lillian for his accompanist. They were not expected to stay in the towns overnight, just sing at the concert hall and catch the late train back to the city. The choirmaster, Henry Stanton, at John's church, St. Mark's, was influential among all the critics in the city, and the papers wrote about him, so people out of town often asked him to recommend a singer. The time they went to Oshawa, Lillian and John wanted to stay together all night but were afraid Mr. Stanton might hear about it. People in the small hotels knew them, since they were advertised as the singer and the pianist from the city, so it was hard to be together for the night in any room in town without someone knowing. But they enjoyed having a lunch in the small restaurant in the town after the concert, people at other tables staring, nudging each other and whispering about the singer and his accompanist from the city. John, clearing his throat loudly, hung up his music case with his coat and looked eagerly at Lillian, her fair hair curled under her small tightly fitting black hat, and the neck of her dress cut low. Her throat was so white and soft that three young fellows at the next table leaned over toward her, hardly talking, looking respectfully at John and mutely at Lillian. For the evening at least John felt they were celebrities, and glancing at Lillian's white throat he said perhaps they ought to take the chance and stay the night at some town hotel. Shaking her head, Lillian said they ought to go back to the city, then to the apartment before he went home.

"Let us not move awhile. Sit there and look at me with your lovely head on one side . . . No, never mind. Move your head. Speak softly to me," he said.

"Silly sweetheart. There. I whispered it. I'll gladly do anything you say, and doing it I'll selfishly get the loveliest, finest feeling I ever have when I don't exist at all and am all a part of you."

"But, you lovely thing, when I sit here looking at your throat . . . Show more of your white throat. Lean toward me."

"I can't lean any farther. The boys at the next table are looking at us and whispering. Go on talking."

"How lovely a white slender throat and the shadow. When I'm looking at your throat like this I get the nervous, restless, helpless feeling and ache all over and then I can see your face with a background of old castles, the Middle Ages – that's it."

"Do I really become so remote from you? You make a dream of it and I never felt so much like flesh and blood."

"No. It's the bridge of your nose. You hardly see anything like it nowadays. I remember a picture of an Italian Madonna with such a profile and hair just that length."

Laughing happily she said: "Then I'll cut my hair and be a modern woman. What will you do then, Troubadour? We'll be out of the opera then."

"Oh, well, I suppose I do sound operatic. I shouldn't sing for a living. People suspect a singer and take everything he says with a grain of salt. It's not necessary that he have any sense, imagination or vitality. Often it's better if he's a bit queer, because he's invariably treated as though he were entirely effeminate. Most of the ones around here are, anyway.

Nothing is expected of me except that I sing well enough. Few of my musical acquaintances are interested in anything but their particular kind of music-making. They don't even get drunk. Were you ever out for an evening with any of them when they were hilarious? They don't have to get drunk as long as they have the company of the ladies. You see how you must sympathize with me and love me in spite of my vocation. Would you love me if I were a plumber, sweetheart?"

"If you were, as you would be, an insistent, greedy, insatiable, lovely plumber. Please don't lean so close to me here."

"I will. I must. I'm an insatiable plumber. There's the lovely smell of you."

"We'll go home and talk about it. Oh, do let's go home."

Though they wanted to stay in the restaurant and have the young fellows and girls staring at them, they hurried and got a bus for the ride back to the city.

Later when John went home, a light was in the room. Paul Ross was waiting for him, stretched out on the bed. Mrs. Errington had said John would return late in the evening and Paul had decided to wait in the room and had fallen asleep on the bed. His feet were resting on the wood at the end of the bed so he would not soil the cover. He still had his coat on, for he had not intended to fall asleep and it was wrinkled at the sleeves. His feet hanging over the end of the bed made him appear extraordinarily tall. The scar on his forehead, a war wound, was a little redder than the rest of the skin on his face. The wound on his forehead was always there to remind him he had left the university to fight in France, and at home again he could not get started decently. He used to talk so much about soldiers' civil reestablishment it always came easily, like a speech, to him, and now he used it as part of his sales talk, selling magazines in the country. For three years he hardly ever talked about the war, but when he became a magazine salesman he carried his two medals in his pocket, showing them to all the women who needed a final persuasive influence. Now he never thought of them as his medals, just a part of his sales talk. The war and the mud in Flanders was all a part of his sales talk.

Waking up, he said to John: "You're looking swell. What have you been doing?"

"A little singing here and there. I was out of town with Lillian tonight."

"How is she? She's a great girl."

"She's looking lovely. How was it for you this trip?"

"Beautiful. The best trip I ever had. I sold them high, wide, and handsome. I put a magazine in every home in the country. I had a line of bull as high as a telegraph pole. I stayed three nights with a farmer's wife whose husband had gone to the city, then sold her the magazine before I left. That's what you call a lack of gallantry. Don't you think? A lack of gallantry on the part of an old soldier, but I told her she'd have the magazine every month for a year to remember me by."

"I hope you weren't waiting for anything in particular all this time. I might have come home earlier."

"I was lying here waiting to talk to you about Fred Thompson. The poor guy. They did hang him after all?"

"It was terrible. It gave me a bad feeling every time I thought about it. You ought to have seen the nervous faces in the crowd around the jail the night before."

"It doesn't make me feel as bad as it might have at one time."

"Why?"

"It was always that way at the war. In the morning you were talking to guys you had known a long time. In the evening they weren't there; all blown to somewhere. They were there, then they weren't there. And you got to the point where they didn't seem to be dead."

"Well, Fred's dead."

"I know. It was something like the time the first fellow you liked got hit. That was very bad, and he seemed absolutely dead; then they all got hit, and it seemed too many of them were dead. It seemed somehow silly to think you couldn't see them again."

"You don't want to go on thinking about it."

"I should forget it, but we were friendly at one time and the way he died seems to bring everything to a head. Everything that was ever good comes suddenly to a head and then it's gone and it's hard to get it straightened out again."

"You make it too personal. I thought about it at the time, and now I don't have to."

"I tell you, you don't have to go to a war to be face to face with death."

"You don't know, you weren't there."

"Fred was closer to me. It's my world, I tell you."

"Maybe. We were in France together. He really was a swell fellow, generous, cheerful, and very fond of the ladies. He used to give a girl the last cent he had and got a big kick out of making her happy. He was violent, quick-tempered and impulsive. Do you remember the days when Fred enlisted, the days of the big recruiting meetings when the sergeants got so much a head and worked all the old stuff on the boys? Fred enlisted right down there in the park with the jail in the corner, at the biggest recruiting meeting ever held in a war time in the city. The park was a natural amphitheatre, and a hundred thousand people were on the hills, and the flatland below was marked out into a track, and the old Indian runner Tom Longboat ran a race with someone who beat him easily. They ha d built a platform and soldiers put on boxing bouts and looked very healthy. In the early evening, with the hundred thousand people on the hills, they set off fireworks that shot across the sky, then they lit torches and the recruiting sergeants began working on the crowd. Fred was there with me, listening to a tough sergeant who was calling young fellows slackers, while old country girls in the crowd got behind young men, pushing them and yelling they could see yellow streaks up their back. Fred was only eighteen then. The sergeant, pointing at him, said he was living a life of ease while boys were dying in France. Some of the old country girls got behind Fred and me, jostling us, urging us to do our bit, while the sergeant bawled hoarsely. And Fred said to the sergeant that if he could punch him on the jaw first, he would have no hesitation about joining the army. The sergeant, coming close to him, shook a finger in his face and Fred punched at him, hitting him. The sergeant started to yell for the police, but Fred offered to join the army and the sergeant said he was a fine fellow and all the girls cheered and put their arms around him, trying to kiss him. It was right down there in the park," Paul said.

"And he looked so simple at the window in the jail."

"I've got a hunch that if he hadn't been at the war he wouldn't have hit that cop. The cop was hurting him and it seemed reasonable to kill him."

"Don't go on making me think about it. What do you want to do now?"

"Walk up to a café and have a sandwich, then go home and get some sleep."

They went downstairs quietly so they wouldn't wake the Erringtons. No one was on the street. It was chilly, almost too cold for a light coat, though the snow wouldn't come till the end of November. They had to walk only a few blocks to the corner café, an open-all-night quick-lunch, and they ordered hot sandwiches and coffee, though John had hardly any appetite. The food had become almost tasteless for him. He had thought he was hungry but could hardly swallow the food: it was just heavy and tasteless. Paul, eating hungrily, ordered another sandwich. John said to him suddenly:

"You know Isabelle Thompson?"

"Fred's sister?"

"Yes."

"I only met her two or three times. She's rather pretty in a very determined way."

"She still is, only she's thin now. She was talking about you."

"I only met her a couple of times."

"I guess she liked you. Phone her, why don't you?"

"What for?"

"Go out with her."

"That's different. She probably took Fred's death pretty hard, didn't she?"

"I can't make her out at all. Once I had a notion she might go in a convent. Instead she finds it necessary to go the other way, as if she has to plunge into the mud and drag everybody with her."

"Don't get excited, and not so loud."

"Oh, well I thought it might be nice if you took her out."

They stopped talking about her. Ross got very jolly and John, laughing happily, tried to hold it in his throat, and then had to open his mouth suddenly and the laugh seemed to come through his teeth. They sat together in the lunchroom smoking and liking each other until it was two o'clock and they were too sleepy to be either shrewd or witty, and neither one was able to laugh at the other, so they paid their checks and went out, standing on the corner till a taxi came along to take Ross home.

John did not see Ross the rest of the week, mainly because he and Lillian were busy arranging the details of a recital they intended to give in Hart House. The recital, to be successful, had to have the patronage of many rich and well-known people in the city, whose names attracted musical critics from all the papers. It was not really the fault of the musical critics that they had this attitude; the editors, John knew from newspaper friends, usually intimated if a recital had any social importance they expected their critic to take advantage of the opportunity to write impressively. The small details of the recital interested Lillian, and they spent many an evening together in her apartment talking excitedly. But she was not really happy. Many small unguarded gestures, when they sat at the table, the light from the reading lamp on her face, expressed her notion of the way a woman ought to act who has a lover and looks forward to being his mistress for a number of years. Moved by a strong feeling she was richly happy, but her emotion had to be advanced beyond a point before she could enjoy the many intimacies that gave her the strong excitement. When John argued, she told him reluctantly it was always in her mind that if she quarreled with him she would go on in the same way of living, only with someone else. She was so lovely, John could not properly express his sympathy, though it seemed more important that she should be easy in her thoughts than that he should be able to go on loving her. Sitting across from her, talking slowly, he tortured himself, sympathizing with her, and was eager to rebuke Isabelle for encouraging her to live in the apartment.

The next time he met her at Lillian's apartment he offered to walk home with her. Her cheerful jauntiness had irritated him when the three of them were talking, and he resented, though he didn't know why, the too vivid red on her lips and the heavy pencil marks on her eyebrows. Her clothes fitted her neatly; her dress was too tight across the hips and under her breasts.

It was almost a straight walk down the long sloping street, the rows of lights undulating on the hill.

"Why did you want Lillian to take the apartment?" he said directly.

"But she wanted something like that, darling."

"You knew that after the first few weeks it would bother her."

"But she loves you and needs something like that."

"It's making her miserable."

"And you're blaming me?"

"You knew it would make her miserable."

For a block they walked and she was hanging heavily on his arm, when she spoke again, holding her lower lip with her teeth. He was astonished to see that she was ready to cry. "Oh, if you only knew how Lillian used to talk about wanting to love you," she said. "She used to talk about it all the time and she merely wanted someone to encourage her." Isabelle's feeling was so sincere he was ashamed of himself and without any words to explain his anger. All the resentment was gone out of him. He felt suddenly friendly. A cold wind was coming up the street from the lake and she held on to his arm tightly. She said: "It was sweet of you to tell Paul Ross to phone me."

"Did he do it?"

"The other night. We went to a show."

"Well, I'd rather see you with him than with Henley."

"That's over," she said abruptly.

They were walking through the old district to Isabelle's house, and under a street lamp two girls dressed jauntily were talking easily with two fellows who had whistled from the other side of the road and crossed over. The slow movements and low laughter of the girls and the fellows under the street lamp made John feel that his conversation with Isabelle was not so very important because he was happier than he had been all evening, simply because he was talking confidentially and walking with Isabelle, who was pretty, along poorly lighted streets in the evening and a wind had come up from the lake blowing strongly against their legs, making them half turn their backs as they held arms.

"Will you come in the house for a while?" she said.

"I will. I'd like to see your mother, too."

So they went into the house together, and Mrs. Thompson, looking clean and tidy, said to John, when Isabelle was upstairs, "Why don't you come oftener, John? I like seeing you."

"I will come."

"I can't get Isabelle to look after herself at all. I'll tell her she'll be in her grave soon and she'll simply shrug her shoulders. I don't like to think of a girl not caring whether she lives or dies." Mrs. Thompson was speaking softly and looking at him intently as if he ought to understand far more than she would be able to express.

"You think she's really not well?"

"I don't know. I seem to be watching her get worse."

"Watching her get worse?"

"It just seems to me that I'm here watching her."

"We're all here watching her."

But he enjoyed the rest of the evening, sitting in the front room talking with Isabelle, who played for him new records, Negro spirituals, on the talking machine. Sometimes she stood in the middle of the floor swaying slowly with the rhythm, and laughing excitedly at the end when she changed the record. Her body did not seem so slim when she moved with so much animation. Her body curved with the rhythm of the music. She was having such a good simple time, amusing herself and him, she went on talking over her shoulder, changing the needle for the disk, explaining about the piece and a dance she had seen on the stage, a Negro whose body was like a strand of rubber, quivering when touched. Laughing gaily she, too, tried to shake her shoulders but couldn't do it, and flushed and tired she sat down.

"Heavens, I'm all in," she said.

"You've been working hard; you oughtn't to do it."

"I've been enjoying myself."

Leaning back, her eyes closed and still breathing heavily, she was smiling, remembering her own pleasure, then opening her eyes quickly she insisted on getting him something to eat.

Before he went home she sat beside him showing him a privately printed book written by a friend of hers, a silly book beautifully printed, written by a man who wrote stories like nursery rhymes and whose mother paid for having them printed, and they laughed, taking turns reading the funny lines.

When he had to go she said, "It was a nice evening, John," and Mrs. Thompson, standing behind her, said: "Come and see me some time, John."

Chapter Eight

*B*y the end of the week John was sure he had been silly and had let thoughts of Isabelle obsess him. It had been just a picture of her in his mind suddenly exciting him, making him restive and nervously alert, and now, knowing the feeling, he could find it silly and was happier, as if it would never be necessary to have such thoughts again. Downtown, in a cafeteria, at the end of the week, he saw Ed Henley sitting across from him, a heavy man, whose shoulders looked too wide when his head was bent down over the table. His head was flat at the top. The hair, a little thin at the crown, suggested an early baldness. Sitting at the table he was simply a dull, heavy-set man who seemed unable to have any thoughts at the moment beyond his food. John, staring at Henley's heavy knuckles and his sloppy lips, was working himself up, almost ready to stand up and shout that Henley was a great pig who liked everything in the world he detested, and was really the idiot who had taken hold first of Isabelle, and indirectly of him. Henley was Isabelle's lover and her good friend. It was over now between them, but he was there, ready to start again. "You fool," John muttered, "you damned idiot." Then he knew Henley had seen him and was trying to speak to him. Without looking up he knew Henley was coming over to sit beside him. "Have you seen Isabelle the last few days?" Henley said, putting his plate of breaded veal cutlets and potatoes au gratin and side dishes of beets and peas on John's table.

"No, I haven't."

"She's gone out of the city."

"Oh."

"Yeah. I don't know where to, either."

"I didn't know she had."

"Well, just between us, Mr. Hughes, I don't think she gave me a very good break." He went on talking about her, his admiration increasing as though she were a famous woman, and it was almost too much to expect that she would go on loving him. "You're a good fellow," John said suddenly, thinking him so simple and honest about his feelings it was almost necessary for them to become confidential. They were both interested in Isabelle, and he knew if he stayed there talking he would be explaining all his own feeling, so he got up hurriedly, still sorry for Henley. "How is it you can eat so much?" he said to him.

"Because I get hungry," Henley said. John kept this answer in his head, on the way along the street, laughing a little; sure that Henley was a simple-minded man.

Even Lillian could not tell him where Isabelle had gone. They were ignorant of her whereabouts till the end of the month, when Paul Ross came back to the city. Paul and John were having a cup of coffee in Childs'. Ross said: "I guess you knew about Isabelle, didn't you?"

"I've been wondering about her. Where is she?"

"She was out of town with me."

"With you?"

"Yes, and listen, John, she's a regular one. Oh, she's a lovely thing. I never knew anything quite like her. There's more excitement in her than in all the women in town."

"I know she's excitable, sometimes a little hysterical."

"It makes no difference. You've never had a woman like her. It left me a bit up in the air."

"What do you mean?"

"I felt I wasn't very important, hardly essential to her excitement. It might just as well have been someone else with her going through the motions. I don't usually feel that way, do I, John? And I ought to be ashamed to admit it now. But not at all. She just burns you up, you or anybody else, a frenzy, a flood and a fire, so I don't feel bad about it."

"Go on."

"Sure. Usually I take them as they come. But there's something ecstatically religious about the release and satisfaction it has for her. I was left outside of it."

"Why do you talk so slowly and smile so stupidly?"

"I just can't help thinking about it, John, that's all. But she can't last long, going like that. It's too bad, because she's so much more than a lovely lady when she's ready, and then there's a curious childish peace for her in her own exhaustion."

"All right, Paul, that's enough. Let it go at that."

"I'm trying to explain the way I felt about an astounding experience. If you're too much of a prig to get the point, I'm sorry for you. Who are you staring at?"

"No one; don't be ridiculous."

"If you want me to shut up I will."

John, looking at him steadily, tried to conceal a quick feeling of anger, and let Paul go on talking about Isabelle till he could hardly understand the words he was using. All the words went into his head but they meant nothing at all to him in combination. "Listen to me," he said suddenly. "That was a hell of a trick."

"But you practically fixed it up for me."

"I didn't; do you hear?"

"You told me she wanted to see me."

"She was a friend of mine and you were a friend of mine, but tell me, what do you think I am? Don't sit there gaping like an idiot, tell me what I am." He leaned forward tensely, waiting for Paul to explain something to him. "You're a fool, that's what you are," Paul said angrily.

"I'm a fool. Yes." He got up at once without finishing his coffee and rushed out the door, leaving Paul, sitting alone, looking after him and thinking he had gone crazy suddenly.

John, calling a taxi, told the driver to take him to Lillian's apartment. On the way up, leaning back in the cab, he got ready all the sentences he intended to use, explaining the matter to Lillian.

In the apartment house he ran up the stairs, opening the door without knocking, rushing into one room and through to another where he heard someone playing the piano. Lillian, standing behind a young girl, one of her few pupils, was watching her touch the keys timidly. The young girl, her mouth open, stared at John and Lillian came to him quickly, pulling him out of the room. "What on earth is the matter with you?" she said. "You look ready to burst a blood vessel."

"You know where Isabelle was all the time?"

"No."

"On the road with Paul Ross."

"Well?"

"And I acted as the pimp for her, do you see? I fixed it all up. I told him she was ready for him, and then they went out on the road together."

"You might have guessed it. After all, it's better she should be with Paul than with the lout Henley."

"No, it isn't. Henley is a simple fellow, but it meant something big to him. It doesn't mean a damn thing to Paul. But that isn't the point. I got him for her and she knew I would feel this way. I'm crazy, am I? Oh, no. I see that part of it, more than you do, more than she does." They were speaking as quietly as possible. Looking between the curtains again at the little girl at the piano, he turned and went out.

CHAPTER NINE

*W*hen snow fell lightly early in December it quickly turned to rain, a slow steady rain. At first it was snow, a few heavy flakes on a very dark day, the flakes melting quickly almost before reaching the sidewalk, and then the rain came heavily, then thinly and steadily, not a good, clean, swift rain. But in the morning when the sun came out and there was a hard frost, the sidewalks were glassy, and little kids on the way to school made slides all along the street to the corner. All the twigs and branches on the trees were coated with thin ice and icicles hung from eavestroughs and the corners of verandas; but then the sun got stronger and the slides were only wet blotches on sidewalks and steam came from the veranda roofs and the ice on the thin branches and twigs began to crack with small snapping sounds and water dripped steadily from the dwindling icicle points, and by midday, when the sun was very strong, there was hardly any frost in the air. The frost had even gone out of the surface earth on the lawns. In the evenings it was cold and hard again and the wind was gusty. It was the wind in the evenings that was cold, and when it was not freezing it was even colder, damp, and heavy, blowing up from the lake.

The wind blew against the window in John's room, rattling it. There were three windows looking out on the street, but the casement of one was loose and he had tightened it with a piece of heavy paper thrust between the sash and the frame. It was nearly ten o'clock in the evening. He had come home early and was reading, glad of the several hours ahead before bedtime, because he liked Marlowe and had reached the second part of *Tamburlaine*, getting excited inside a little when there was a rush and flow of words. The excitement in the characters and in the author was in John because of the swing and rush of the words. Sometimes the characters in the book hardly seemed important as long as he caught some of the author's feeling of exultation in the splendor of his own images. It was better for John, alone in the house, for there were no noises in other rooms. Mrs. Errington and her husband had gone out a little late in the evening.

He was lying on the bed reading and dusting ashes from his cigarette, which had fallen on the page. He heard someone knocking on the door downstairs. Whenever he was alone in the house and someone knocked on the door, he answered, so now he went downstairs and opened the front door. Isabelle, her hand out to him, stepped into the hall.

"I wanted to see you, John."

"You can't see me here."

"Yes I can, the people went out about half an hour ago."

"I don't want to see you at all."

"Lillian told me that."

"Where were you now?"

"On the other side of the street watching the light in your room." She was still shivering, for she had on only a light fawn coat and the red felt hat. It was a pretty coat, but now she had the thin collar turned up and her nose was red. Outside it was frosty and she looked very thin and cold in the light coat.

"Why on earth didn't you wear a heavy coat?" he said irritably.

"This one looks better. My heavy coat's worn and funds are getting low."

Standing in the hall, under the light, smiling a little, she felt warmer and began to turn down the collar of her coat, all the time looking at him steadily, aware that he intended asking her to sit down in Mrs. Errington's front room. It became so clear to him that she was sure of his thoughts, he expressed his sudden exasperation by saying: "Come on upstairs and sit down in my room a few minutes. You'll have to be out soon or the Erringtons will be home."

Upstairs she took off her coat at once and resentfully he watched her looking around the room carefully. His fingers were fumbling with the neckband of his shirt as though he ought to have a collar and tie on. She sat down on the one chair in the room. He sat down on the bed.

"Well," he said.

"It was getting quite cold out."

"You'll have pneumonia."

"Probably. It'll soon be Christmas."

"Is that what you came to tell me, Isabelle?"

"No. That's just a fatalistic observation, John, dear. I know how you feel about me and it makes me feel broken up and I simply had to see you. I had to see you alone and you had told Lillian to keep me away from you."

She was talking so patiently and smiling so wistfully, he couldn't help feeling that in some way he had misbehaved, and she was there to make it all a matter for explanation, so he gave her a cigarette, his face absolutely expressionless to indicate a sudden impartial feeling. He said he was glad she had come to see him.

"Why did you resent me going off with Paul Ross?"

"I didn't. It hurt me to have to procure him for you."

"But don't you see how I felt?. The way my brother had been killed made me feel I could never be any good and for all other people I would be pretty low. It wasn't my fault, and I resented it because there was something fine about Fred. Wasn't there something fine about him, John? And the way he died had nothing to do with my feeling for him, only I knew I would have to go on with that feeling of personal degradation. As far as everybody else is concerned I'm degraded. I went on thinking of myself in that way till I was almost eager for more of it, wanting to hurt myself. See, I know just the way it was with me. So it was easy just letting myself go with Ed Henley because he loved me for a kind of ill-fame attached to me, and in his slow way he had it figured out I ought to be easy. I am, only I want to take everything along with me." She had got more excited holding on to the arms of the chair, staring at him while he shook his head, eager to tell her how sorry he was for her. "Wasn't it better to go from Henley to Paul?"

"No, he won't bother about you at all."

"You don't know him. He's really down and out now, but can you imagine it, he wanted to be an architect, then the war got him. Did you know that? The war got him and someday he'll start thinking more intensely and it will be bad for somebody. I felt that about him and it was almost good for us to be together. I mentioned him to you because you and Lillian are the only friends I've got."

Then she said it was probably wrong for her to mention it at all, for he was, in a way, apart from it, since he was becoming fairly successful with his music. Lillian and he could look forward to so much happiness, they were really altogether beyond her.

"That thought's a mania with you," he said angrily.

"But it's true just the same."

"It isn't, I tell you. I love Lillian and she loves me, but we both want to be good friends with you."

"But sometimes you seem so much of a prig."

"You're not fair to me."

"You didn't used to have that quality, but I've watched it growing in you."

"Don't be nasty, Isabelle. Be nice. Have a smoke."

"What were you reading?" she said, picking up the book. "Do you really like the Elizabethans?"

"Mainly Marlowe."

"I used to like them, too, but it's too gaudy a performance for me now. Too much upholstering, I suppose. It hasn't anything to do with my life. But I thought you were interested only in . . . ."

"In music, you were going to say."

"Yes."

"I know I'm always apologizing for liking anything else. It seems to be almost an indecent offence against the standards."

"No. I didn't mean that. I used to like reading, but now it all passes beyond me. I can only see the words on the page; it never really touches me at all now. How quiet it is in the room here and from the window, looking out, the streets seem so silent, though they are cold, and the streetlight so steady. It's too late in the year now, but a month or so ago I used to watch the streetlight not far away from my upstairs window and for a long time I could faintly see the insects crawling on the white glass shade. I used to have to keep looking hard. It was like that, late at night, when I had most of my thoughts about you, and wanted to see you . . . . Well, I used to like reading, that's what we were talking about, but every time I sit down now with a book it all becomes a very silly, trifling exercise of the imagination with me sitting there ready to toss away the book, always feeling my own thoughts so much stronger and alive and restless . . . ."

"Talk quietly. Even now your face glows and your eyes are wild and your voice rises."

For a time she sat without moving, hardly aware he was in the room. The long silence was awkward and he hoped for some slight noise in the house or on the street that might hold his attention. The street was quiet, then he heard some-one starting an automobile farther down, but after a few sec-onds could hardly follow the sound of wheels and the engine, and the street was quiet again.

"Lillian would probably have married Fred if he had lived," she said.

"What's that?"

"She was more in love with him than she imagined, and they would have got married when he was ready."

"Dear Isabelle," he said considerately, "why do you say that?"

"I say simply the shock of his arrest and his death mixed up her feeling for him, but later on she will see the way it was."

"I tell you, you're raving mad."

"No, I still have some feeling for you."

"I wish you hadn't, then."

"John, kiss me once and I'll go."

A stupid smile was on his face and he shook his head awkwardly as if not hearing her. Getting up quickly she put her hands on his head before he could move and kissed him tightly, and when he was still looking at her, only getting up slowly, backing away, she leaped at him, kissing him fiercely on the neck, hanging on to him tightly. Hanging on to him, her body was tense and he felt her heart beating against him and all the muscles of her arms and legs quivering and straining. She was very slim and hardly soft at all, but when tense, her slimness made her more nervous, and he felt it all in her. He put his arms around her, kissing her, hardly breathing because it seemed all his feelings for Isabelle that had been mixed up where concentrated into a sudden intensity of emotion, finding a release only in holding on to her. Some of the nervous tenseness in her passed to him and he trembled all over. He felt his heel pattering on the floor, and desperately pressed down on it to hold his legs steady. "I've got to love you," he said. The one expression on her face remained there all the time, only her eyes seemed to get brighter.

When they lay down, first of all, she hardly said anything. She didn't smile at him and they didn't pet each other at all, just sought the one swift feeling, then she closed her eyes, lying on the bed.

It was over for both of them quickly and standing up he said: "I don't know why I did that."

"Don't you?"

"No."

"Do you want me to go?"

"Yes."

"Are you sorry I came?"

"Yes."

She was not offended and even smiled a little, sitting down, putting on her hat. A mirror was over the dresser in the corner of the room and she moved her head from side to side following it in the glass. Still watching, John was anxious to say something that would sound decently appropriate, but could only go on looking at her. Suddenly he said: "You were all wrong about Lillian and Fred."

"Oh, no."

"I wish you'd admit that you were."

All his senses were alert and he heard the faintest noises outside on the street. Quite clearly he heard voices no farther away than the nearest lamppost and the voices came a little closer. He heard Mr. and Mrs. Errington talking to each other.

"Please, please, Isabelle," he said picking up her coat and trying to drape it around her shoulders. Hurrying, she took time to say she couldn't run out with her coat draped around her shoulders. Rapidly she left the room and he followed her to the top of the stairs; from there he could look down and out of small glass windows in the door, beyond the veranda, down the walk to the street. Mr. and Mrs. Errington had not turned up the walk yet and he felt if Isabelle could get to the door it would be all right, if only they didn't look through the glass and see her coming downstairs. Hearing her opening the door he turned quickly, walking back to his room, hardly moving, listening for sounds on the veranda, underneath his room. Isabelle said something quietly, then Mr. Errington spoke and he heard Mrs. Errington talking. The conversation was short, but trying so hard to hear the words, wishing she would go, it seemed to him to last a long time It was over and Isabelle's high heels tapped on the sidewalk. From the window he saw her hurrying along the street. Her coat collar was turned up, she was under the lamppost, holding her hand at her throat. The sidewalks were dry again and the wet spots, hardening, were slippery. The light from the streetlamp shone on a slippery spot on the sidewalk.

He simply lay down on the bed, waiting. Downstairs in the hall the Erringtons talked quietly, then they went into the kitchen and a kettle rattled on a stove. They were going to have a cup of tea and talk about it before coming upstairs. For John, lying in the bed, everything had become calm and it was hard to believe he had been excited a few moments ago, for now the Erringtons were the only people in the world for him and every movement of theirs in the kitchen was important.

Finally they came upstairs, Mr. Errington following his wife. They went into their room and, undressing very quietly, got into bed. Usually they read the papers in bed, and when John came home in the evenings he heard the papers rustling on their bed and the light was always in the room. Sometimes they quarreled steadily, but it never seemed to prevent them reading the papers. Coming up the stairs in the evenings late at night and always hearing the sounds in their bedroom, John had got to like them, feeling he knew all about them and their lives. Listening now, waiting nervously, he was attached to all sounds, wanting earnestly that nothing should disturb them and every night he should be able to hear them, since they were a part of his own life around the house.

Tonight, they did not read the papers, but undressed quietly and got into bed and began to talk steadily. When Mr. Errington raised his voice, he suddenly lowered it, as though she had nudged him. They talked quietly almost an hour and John, trying so hard to hear a phrase, a few words, tired himself out and fell asleep on the bed without undressing.

Chapter Ten

*I*n the morning Mrs. Errington, getting him his breakfast hardly spoke till he was finished. Reluctantly, she sat down and said: "I wanted to talk to you about the young woman, Miss Thompson, who was here last night."

"Yes, Mrs. Errington."

"Well, Mr. Errington told me to tell you that you ought to leave at the end of the week."

"I will."

"I'm sorry."

She was so sorry he would have to go she was ready to explain it was her husband who had urged her to give him notice without even asking for an explanation. It never even occurred to him to try and argue with her. She was a plump, friendly woman, who had been so respectable all her life such an escapade excited her and aroused her sympathy, although it could not be tolerated. So she sat at the end of the table, looking at him a little wistfully, determinedly expressing by her attitude approval of her husband's opinion. All her good nature and the restraint of the years, so uneventful for her, trying to be interested in her husband's reform politics, when younger, and sure she would someday encounter a strong lasting excitement, then missing it and thinking of it a little bashfully, without any hope, gave her now a kindly feeling, urging her to comfort him even though her common sense prompted her to hold aloof.

"It really would be better for you to go without talking about it at all, don't you think?" she said, her voice lifting a little as she leaned forward, half expecting he would be unable to resist telling her something. If he had suddenly started to cry, expressing in some way a fresh and violent emotion, it would have been awkward for both of them, for she would have put her arms around him. Mrs. Errington was about forty-five, her hair still dark, and hardly any lines were in her plump fresh face. They weren't saying a word to each other, thought they were both sharing the same feeling and perhaps some of the same thoughts.

"You're quite right, Mrs. Errington," he said abruptly, standing up.

"What's that?"

"Mr. Errington is quite right." Turning before going into the front room to the piano, he said: "Would you mind telling me how you knew the young lady's name was Thompson?"

"She told us. That's what makes it worse. It wouldn't do at all for us, if people got to know about it. We knew you had been a friend of the family."

In the front room, as though nothing had happened at all, he stood at the piano, sounding notes with one hand, going over the scales three or four times, while Mrs. Errington, moving behind in the other room, cleared the dishes off the table. She had never objected to giving him a late breakfast. Sometimes she had offered to have a cup of tea with him. John was not even thinking of asking her husband for an explanation. Mr. Errington was merely her husband, a social democrat, a prohibitionist and an advanced liberal, though really a hard puritan living on a vicarious excitement he got out of such ideas. John had always liked him, not wanting him to be any other way.

Outside in the early afternoon, he was uncertain whether to see Lillian or to phone Isabelle, and went downtown to waste the afternoon hours in the arena, seeing the hockey teams practice on the artificial ice. The players, in bright sweaters, were always formed in shifting patterns on the ice surface and it was easy following them, wondering how to explain to Lillian that he was leaving the Erringtons. Once he thought of Isabelle. The palms of his hands started to sweat. He began to talk out loud, resentfully, then he was puzzled, hardly thinking of her at all. In the arena, leaning over the rail he watched a college team practice on the ice. Most of the players wore old sweaters with holes torn in them. The forwards worked smoothly together, almost ready now to start the league season. The ice was in bad condition, cut up, heavily ridged, because teams had been practicing on it all day.

In the evening he went to St. Mark's Church to practice with the choir. Usually all the singers talked together in two rooms in the vestibule at the back of the church before Stanton went to the organ. John was not popular with the choirmen or other soloists, who thought he only sang in the church for the sake of money.

Mr. Stanton, well dressed, his face red and shining, came over and stood beside John, clearing his throat brusquely, and rubbing his hand uneasily down the side of his face, holding his head at an angle. He raised his eyebrows, indicating he was about to speak delicately. John smiled at him. Stanton was confused before he started.

"I'd like to talk to you privately, John."

"Of course, Mr. Stanton."

They moved over to the far corner of the room, and other soloists and choirmen looked at them suspiciously, sure some favor, forever eluding them, was being granted to John.

"The truth is I have something delicate to say, John."

"Of course, Mr. Stanton."

"You understand, I wouldn't say it, only the minister, Doctor Ellwood, has instructed me to say it."

"Please tell me. What is it?"

"He wants you to quit here."

"Why?"

"He's heard things about you, shall I say, detrimental to your good reputation, that he – should I go on?"

"If you don't mind."

"Well, it's about the Thompson girl, the one whose brother was executed a few months ago. Doctor Ellwood has heard you've been carrying on with her in the house where you've been staying and that people have complained."

"Tell me one thing first," John said. "Who told him this? Was it Isabelle Thompson? It wasn't, was it? It couldn't have been, could it? Was it Mrs. Errington?"

"No. Maybe I oughtn't to tell you, but a Mr. Errington phoned and said he believed Doctor Ellwood ought to know."

"Oh, well, then, I see."

"Tell me, John. Is it true?"

"Why, Miss Thompson happened to call on me last night when the Erringtons were out and was just leaving when they came in."

"Is there anything between you and Miss Thompson?"

"Eh?"

John looking at him a little stupidly, began to laugh. People at the other side of the room glanced at them. "I wish you could tell me that," he said, laughing again, only there was no flow at all, he seemed to be having such a hard time getting his breath. "I wish you'd tell me," he said, staring at Stanton, who was getting redder in the face, coughing to express his irritation. Mr. Stanton went on talking, but John was hardly listening; the muscles in his jaws were moving and he was pale. Mr. Stanton, believing he was experiencing a strong emotion because of losing his position, felt sorry for him.

"It would be different," he said, "if this wasn't a church. Do you want me to make any representations to Doctor Ellwood?"

"Do you think it would do any good?"

"No. You know how intolerant all his moral sermons are every Sunday."

"Then I'll resign."

"To make it easier, Doctor Ellwood thinks you could have a month's pay now instead of waiting till the end of the month."

"I won't bother practicing here tonight. I'll go at once."

"That was pretty decent of him paying you for a month, don't you think?"

"I must go at once, there's something important . . ."

"I mean it's decent of him, knowing what he's like."

Mr. Stanton followed John into the cloakroom, gravely insisting they had always been good friends, and that aside from personal matters, he had a high opinion of his voice. John was not listening, throwing his scarf around his neck and pulling on his coat, so Mr. Stanton became desperately determined to make it clear that his voice, if further developed, and trained, assured him of a fine career. Following John to the door, he stood outside on the stone step, shouting: "You ought to go to another city, do you hear, you ought to go to Europe."

John was hurrying down the street to the corner, looking for a pay telephone. The sidewalks were slippery in spots and twice he tripped, recovering his balance abruptly, and he slowed down because it occurred to him, thinking of himself almost as another personality, that nothing would be more ridiculous than to fall on the sidewalk in such a temper. It would break the mood; there would be a loss of energy; so he walked carefully as far as the corner drugstore. Three young men, loafing in the lighted entrance, were giggling and whistling faintly at a tall girl who had crossed the street.

In the drugstore he waited till a fat woman came out of the phone booth. The proprietor of the store smiled at him politely, hoping he might buy something, and John stared, eager to insult him. The woman came out of the both. John went in and phoned Isabelle. She answered.

"It's John," he said at once. "Look here, there's a limit, do you hear? I've got to move away from Errington's and I've just lost my job in the church." He was talking so rapidly and loudly the clerk in the store peered at him through the window. Becoming calm suddenly, he realized Isabelle could not understand anything he was saying and explained quietly that he had lost his job.

"Oh, what a pity," she said.

Telling her about the Erringtons, he said abruptly: "How did you come to tell them your name?" and expected her to pause. At once she said: "I thought it would be best. I was polite to them. Introduced myself. I told them that I called to see you because I couldn't get in touch with you. What could I say there on the veranda?"

"I don't know."

"What would you have done?"

"I don't know."

"You wanted me to stay."

"All right. Tell me, what'll I tell Lillian?"

His hand, holding the earpiece, trembled a little, and she said finally: "Tell her I called for you at the church once or twice and they knew too much about me. Blame it on me. It was my fault anyway and Lillian won't mind, and tell her you're moving because you want a cheaper place now you've lost your job."

"But what'll I do?"

"Dear John. It's a shame. Oh, if only I really could help you." She was speaking sincerely and he knew at the moment she was anxious to help him. He said suddenly, "Damn you," and hung up the phone.

In the cab, on the way to Lillian's apartment, he tried to make up a story that would sound plausible. This was not easy, because he was thinking mainly of Isabelle.

Entering Lillian's apartment he thought he was smiling normally, talking casually. Lillian had on a dressing gown and her hair was held back tightly behind her ears. She said quickly: "What on earth is the matter with you?"

"Why do you ask that?"

"You look so pale and you're grinning weirdly."

"I'll tell you then," he said casually, taking off his coat and sitting down. "The truth is that I've lost my position at the church. What do you think of that? Of course, I don't need to leave till the end of the month, but I thought I'd quit at once."

"But why?"

"I'm a bad character. At least they didn't like the people of quality who called for me at the church. You and Isabelle had been there several times, and mainly because of Isabelle, who is getting known, I guess, they got the notion I was not the right kind of a character to sing every Sunday in the church." It did not sound sincere. It sounded as if he had hardly said it at all, and Lillian simply looked at him, her mouth opening, while she slowly raised her right hand. John thought she was going to burst out laughing. Instead, she nodded her head and said suddenly: "Of course that's silly, but don't you see what's happened? Someone told some church people about you and me and this apartment and just like such people, they feel that they can't go on employing you in the church." Then she started to cry, muttering that sooner or later some ill-luck had to come to them, and working herself up gradually, finally declared passionately that all her thoughts for days had been confused and she sometimes wondered why she loved him at all. Her feeling had changed and was all for herself. Then she said quietly: "Poor Isabelle. Do you wonder she is almost obsessed by the notion that we've left her, when even those church people mention her?"

"Now, don't make a martyr out of her."

"I believe you hate her."

"Right now I'm tired of thinking of her. I'm going home."

"But I want to talk about her."

"Well, I'm going home."

It was a long walk home from the apartment, south, then across the viaduct, and he was glad of the frosty air and the necessity of rapid walking to keep warm. Losing the position in the church was not the same as losing a job in an office or a store. In the city there were many offices and stores, and some jobs were much alike, only the employers were a little different. In the whole city there were only two or three church soloist positions with decent salaries. A man having one of these positions had the prestige and support of people who were influential. It was hardly any use trying to be a good singer in the city if you did not have the approval of the influential people, who all worked together as though belonging to the same lodge. If you had one of the positions and lost it because of some personal antipathy, then the other good churches were closed to you, and smaller ones paid about twenty dollars a month. It was like losing a membership in a socially important club.

But John, on the way home, starting to cross the bridge, was tired thinking of positions he could not have, and was anxious to get home to his room in Errington's house. It had been a fine, sun-lit room in the north side of the house, and in the morning, after watching kids playing in the street, he could go down and have a late breakfast with Mrs. Errington, who sometimes had a cup of tea with him while gossiping pleasantly about all the neighbors, who had become so well known to him, he often spoke to one on the street without really knowing her at all. Every night he had walked across the bridge on the way home from work at the church. He was on the second span of the wider bridge over the big valley, and the line of lights was straighter. Directly ahead, on the other side of the valley, green and golden lines of light flashed and faded and flashed again in electric signs on building tops. Below, in the ravine, the Don River was frozen over with a thin coating of ice. He stopped walking, leaning against the stone, looking down the valley at the rows of lights in the part to the south, where all the flatland would be flooded in the spring when the Don overflowed its banks. The park lights were always in the same regular patterns. On the right side of the valley on the slope of the hill was a cemetery and a line of trees, a row of flat-roofed houses, lights in the windows, farther back from the cemetery, and light streaks in the sky behind the line of trees with bare branches. Far down at the south of the park in the corner, though he could not see it now, was the jail on the hill where the crowd had gathered, singing the songs and looking at the window.

CHAPTER ELEVEN

*H*e moved at the end of the week to a three-dollar-a-week room on Bond Street, close to the downtown section of the city. The landlady, Mrs. Stanley, who had iron-gray hair piled high on her head, was a widow who owned three houses in a row on the street. She had lost most of her lower teeth. Three, yellow at the gums and high and narrow, flashed every time she drew back her lower lip, smiling at John, a sober-looking young man, stocky and sensible, who wanted the cheapest room she had. Standing at the window of the room, almost facing the old brick cathedral on the other side of the street, and the public garage a little way down the lane, she told him, whispering hoarsely, that the man in the next room, a Mr. Gibbons, was a communist, but quiet and decent in every other way. It was something he ought to know, she thought. The room was in poor condition when he first saw it, and smelled of gas. On Monday when he came again the walls had been freshly papered and clean curtains hung at the windows, but the room still smelled of gas.

The first night there he lay awake, sure he was going to be poor and thinking with disgust of all kinds of poverty. Though he had saved almost fifteen hundred dollars, he had the feeling if he spent any of it he would never go away to have his voice trained. Since losing the job at the church he had made up his mind never to bother any more with church work, and yet did not want to sing the songs that he would have to sing in the popular theaters.

Lillian came in the afternoon to see his room, and sitting in two old-fashioned chairs, after they had opened the windows wide to let the cold air into the room, they decided they could not go on with his recital, now they could no longer count on the enthusiasm of Mr. Stanton and Doctor Ellwood, or any church people. Lillian was sorry, though hardly talking about it, looking out the window across the road.

"What are you going to do?" she said.

"Get a job."

"Whereabouts?"

"I don't know. I want to get some more money."

"Maybe that's better."

She was politely interested, sympathizing with his ambition, though it was hardly a part of her own plan. Lazily she was looking out the window. No one was on the street. Someone was hammering, steel on steel, in the garage down the lane. There was nothing outside to interest her. She was not trying to suggest, by her lack of strong feeling, that she had lost some of her love for him; only there was hardly any emotional intensity behind her words. Unexpectedly she said, glancing at him and smiling: "You needn't worry about Isabelle bothering you anymore."

"Why?"

"She's in bed very sick."

"What's the matter with her?"

"A very bad cold and probably the flu, too. I was there last night."

"Well, listen, don't even talk about me to her, will you?"

A little amused by his sincerity, and to humor him she said: "Of course I won't if you don't want me to." Puzzled now, she said quietly: "It was almost a disease with you."

He merely shrugged his shoulders, refusing to talk.

At night, in bed it was lonely, the familiar sounds in the Errington house were not there, the noises outside on the street were strange, and cars going into the garage kept him awake. The noises kept him wide awake and he wanted to go to sleep instead of lying, talking to himself about Isabelle.

In the morning he went downtown to the employment office of the big store where he had worked before, and after sitting there two hours they said they weren't hiring anybody; they had taken on many clerks for the Christmas business and it would be a slack time afterward.

At one of the radio stations they promised him some work after Christmas.

So he was settling down after an intense emotional experience, satisfied to remember he loved Lillian, and would go away and come back for her. Every plan he made provided for a return to the city to marry Lillian. In the daytime he saved money eating at armchair lunches so they could have cheap seats in the theaters.

Planning his future so steadily, he forgot all about Hobson, his music master, and thinking of him, it seemed foolish to go on paying for a training leading mainly into church work. Early in the evening he went to Hobson's house and told him he wouldn't take any more lessons because he wanted to go away and didn't believe such lessons would help him. They started to argue and John was glad Mrs. Hobson wasn't there to offer him sandwiches and tea. Hobson, who was friendly with all the critics, and successful training church singers, wanted John to give the recital because a performance by one of his pupils usually turned out all right. Unable to understand why John had left the choir at St. Mark's, he insisted he go on and give the recital, calling him many names rapidly. Hobson was a fat man, whose face got red and blue when angry, and he breathed slowly afterward, as though recovering from a fit. It was not a good time for John to tell him he had had enough oratorio singing, and wanted to study opera in another country.

When John spoke so frankly, Hobson began to breathe slowly, his face gradually assuming a natural color, and he said with dignity: "I can do no more for you. Please go."

"What would you advise me to do?"

"Do as you think best and ruin your voice."

Out on the street again, looking back at the red-brick house and the light in the front window, John had a feeling of exultation. So many thoughts came into his head rapidly he had no one definite impression, just the fine feeling that he was stripping himself of every tie holding him to the one spot. Walking along, his breath was steaming. It was the time of the first heavy fall of snow and it had got colder, remaining cold all week, and the snow kept on falling. The garage man in the lane was doing little business because automobiles would not turn along the lane: it was too hard getting out again. The wheels of the cars spun ineffectually, the snow spraying against the board fence. The snow spattered into the garage, falling on the shoulders of the garage man, standing there, hatless, an unlighted cigar in his mouth. John stood under the light, his hands over his ears, watching the man in the automobile get out and look contemptuously at the garage man, who shrugged his shoulders, implying that it was a long lane and he could not be expected to be cleaning it all day while snow was falling. Two older men passed wearing earlugs underneath their hats and two little kids, sliding on the street, laughed at them. A long time ago everybody in the city used to wear earlugs in the cold weather, but now they believed the winters got milder every year, and went around the street, their ears red and swollen, their breath steaming.

John, standing by the light, saw Mr. Gibbons, who roomed in the same house, coming down the street. Mrs. Stanley had hinted that Gibbons, the communist, ought to be avoided, but he had a pleasant smile and was anxious to be friendly. They walked up the street together, beginning a silly argument. John had suggested everybody ought to be wearing colored toques, which would not only be warmer and comfortable, but would be more colorful on the streets. Gibbons, with humor, insisted the idea had no utility, and no one would be any better off, leaving an impression that John had been silly, because it was a cold night and necessary to make a conversation walking up the street.

John asked Gibbons to sit in his room the rest of the evening. They might first of all go out and get a bottle of wine, he suggested, but Gibbons explained he never drank. John asked if he had taken a vow in chastity as well as abstinence in the holy order of communism. They both laughed politely.

"I've nothing against girls," Gibbons said, "only they don't appeal to me at all."

"Don't you ever go out with them?"

"No. They just don't appeal to me. Once when we were having a convention out West the fellows put a woman in my room, but I didn't get sore. They thought it was a fine joke."

"Don't you ever want them at all?"

"I never even think about them."

"What do you do then?"

"I mean I like women well enough, only I never have to think of them in that way."

"Supposing you had a lovely woman here now?"

"It would be all right for you, but it wouldn't mean anything to me. It's silly the way men are always giving themselves to women, don't you think so?"

"Maybe you're right."

"Oh, I know I am. I figured it out a long time ago and it's easy for me now because I haven't any feeling for them."

Gibbons began to talk about the communist movement in the city. They hadn't had a chance, he said, since the trouble following the war. The time would come. There was absolutely no doubt about that. It was his opinion, though some in the party did not agree with him, they ought to take advantage of every gathering caused by a minor disturbance. Talking slowly, he was determined to express all his thoughts clearly, frowning heavily. "For example," he said, "do you remember the big crowd that gathered around the jail the night before they hanged that fellow Thompson? We ought to have been able to do something about it. The crowd was sore at the police and ready for trouble. It might have been used in some way, because it moves everybody."

"Go on, what do you mean?"

"A hanging draws everybody into it. We're all held. It takes hold of some stronger than others. Some are sentimental and some are hard, but they're all crucified in their own way. Didn't it get you?"

"I couldn't get away from it."

"That's it. Of course Thompson was of no importance, but we ought to have been able to take advantage of the disturbance."

"You think he was of no importance?" John said angrily.

"Generally speaking, I mean. Did you know him?"

"I did."

"Well, I knew him when we were in the army. You could not do anything with him. That was before he was an officer. He was apt to be enthusiastic, but more often cynical. I was sorry for him, but he couldn't really affect anybody."

"I had a good opinion of him."

"Yeah, I think we ought to have been able to do something about it. It's not important whether he was Fred Thompson or Jack Spratt . . . ."

"I say it is of the utmost importance. Do you hear?"

"My God man, we shouldn't quarrel about something like that. You resent it, eh? Let me tell you, then, he was indifferent to any cause. He would have laughed or sneered at any movement, and was the worst enemy of any kind of political progress."

"Shut up do you hear?" John said, leaning toward him, holding on tightly to the edge of the table. "Shut up, do you hear?" Gibbons, puzzled, shook his head awkwardly. "If you're a relative of his, I'm sorry," he said. "I was just speaking of men generally, and meant I couldn't conceive of his life or death having any lasting effect . . . ."

"Oh, stop talking. For God's sake, shut up . . . . You won't eh?" He reached over suddenly and slapped Gibbons across the face, then stared at him stupidly, surprised at what he had done. Gibbons stood up, drawing in his breath with a whistling noise between his teeth, too astonished to control further the muscles of his body. Before he could move at all John said, "Oh, Lord, I'm awfully sorry. I'm so sorry. You must forgive me. I was hardly listening to what you were saying. The words, I mean. Talking about him and thinking about the whole thing excited me and I wanted to stop talking. I hardly know what you were saying about him. Forgive me." He held out his hand smiling.

"Well, if it was that way."

"It was. I assure you."

"All right, then." They shook hands smiling, embarrassed, and started to make a new conversation. Gibbons talked to John about Trotsky, one of the few great men in the world, he said, who would eventually return to Russia when the Red Army needed a leader. There was no argument, and talking lazily, they felt sleepy.

John was undressed, ready to turn out the light, when Gibbons, in his dressing gown, came into the room again. He was worried and anxious to make an explanation.

"You remember we were talking about girls?" he said.

"Yes. That's all right."

"No, I was thinking about it over there in my room. I don't want you to get me wrong."

"No, it's all right."

"But there's nothing wrong with me. I don't want any stories getting around. I just don't like women," he said and smiled apologetically, closing the door quietly.

CHAPTER TWELVE

*I*n the holiday week at Christmas, Lillian went to her par-
ents' home in the country. John was alone. In the city at
Christmas time a young fellow in a rooming house without
a plan for the holiday is really alone.

Gibbons, in the same house, was alone, too, but it did not
bother him. The holiday enthusiasm was an illusion he said
to John. By refusing to spend money on Christmas presents
he did not contribute to the economic prosperity of dealers
who fostered the illusion. It sounded so entirely reasonable,
John felt good-humored.

On Christmas Day, deciding to have a fine elaborate meal
in the most expensive hotel in the city, he hesitated for a long
time, thinking of the price and the extravagance, and assuring
himself he was becoming a miser. Finally, in the evening,
he walked down to the hotel. The lobby was crowded, everybody prosperous, many fat men stood there in fur coats and
derby hats, smoking cigars.

In the dining room, before he had ordered, sitting alone
at the white table, he did not get the warm tingling feeling
of satisfaction he had expected. It was all a little silly, because
he was not very hungry. The lights were bright, the trays
passing all had fine rich-smelling food on them, but he was
hardly hungry. Looking around the room he saw a priest, well
dressed and carefully shaved, sitting a few tables away from
him, his head bent down, a little bald on the top. The priest

was eating slowly, enjoying a fine meal, all by himself in the crowded hotel dining room. John, recognizing Father Mason, got up quickly and went over to shake hands with him. The priest, glad to talk with someone, invited John to sit down at his table. "My housekeeper wanted to go home," he said, "and I let her. I'm a little tired of her cooking anyway. I have the same dishes too often. She was sorry for me, thinking I'd be all alone, and all the time I was thinking I'd come here for the dinner. She's a dear soul, though." His breath smelt of liquor and he was feeling very jolly. He was thinner and his clothes hung on him loosely. His face was red, almost feverish. Since he had had something to drink, it was hard to know whether he was in good health. All the time now he had a fever, he said, and was thinking of going to Europe for a few months because he had lost twenty pounds. Often he had to change his clothes four times a day, from the fever and the sweating. That was all that was wrong with him and he expected to live to be eighty. He asked John about his singing and learned he had lost his job at St. Mark's Church. "You're better off anyway. Why did you want to sing there?" he said. A bigoted remark occurred to him, but he was too good-natured to express it. "Oh, well, this is good food here," he said.

So they had a splendid dinner, enjoying the rich food and encouraging each other to talk. When they were finished Father Mason said: "Are you doing anything tonight?"

"Nothing at all. I was thinking of a show."

"Oh forget that. We ought to have a little drink together in a place where it's quiet."

"The lady at my rooming house will sell us a bottle of Scotch at any time. She never put it to me that way, but said if I was ever in need of it she'd help me out."

They walked up Yonge Street together, their feel crunching on packed-down snow not yet shoveled from the sidewalk. Tall flat surfaces of office buildings were clean and untouched by snow. It was a holiday night, but lights were in the rectangular windows high up in the buildings.

In his room, John, smelling the gas, had to open the windows, though Father Mason said he could not smell it at all. That was the trouble, at first you could not smell it, and then, once the odor was detected, you seemed to smell it all the time. Father Mason sat down away from the window, out of the draft, for fear of getting a cold, it was so easy for him to sweat, and John went downstairs to get a bottle of whiskey.

They had several drinks, John waiting for Father Mason to get more hilarious, but the priest sat there, hardly talking till he said suddenly: "I don't care when I die. I'm ready to die at any time. It will be easy for me and I don't expect it to bother me at all, just let me go to confession and get everything cleared up. I don't care when I die."

"Are you feeling the draft from the window?"

"No, when I get hot. I don't feel the cold at all."

"I'll close it anyway."

"All right. Have you seen Isabelle Thompson recently?" the priest said.

"She's been sick, I think. I saw her a while ago, but she's been sick."

"I know she's sick. I think she thought she was going to die." Father Mason was talking slowly, soberly, hardly looking at John, his eyes turned to the other side of the room. His forehead was sweating, for he had been drinking a great deal during the day and was finding it difficult to avoid talking too rapidly about thoughts now bothering him. He wanted to make everything sound reasonable and detached, but his feeling was getting too strong.

"Women are funny that way. They are like vats of wine. Tap them and they get started and flow on till they're finished," he said.

"That's not bad, either."

"No. I'd be that way myself if I ever got started, but – nonsense. I never think of them at all now. Do you?"

"All the time."

"It was bad enough the way Fred died," Father Mason said.

"It was awful."

"It was harder on me than I ever let anyone know, walking with him to the rope. I knew him well, that was the trouble. You believe, don't you, that I don't care at all when I die?"

"Yes, only I don't feel that way."

"I've been trying for a long time to forget Fred. I don't ever want to walk to the scaffold with anybody, though I'll probably have to do it, because they'll have a hard time getting anyone else. The main thing is, I've been trying not to think. The drink helps a bit there." He poured himself another drink and took it easily, hardly feeling it at all in his throat. "I like the taste of whiskey," he said, "but I drink too much of it."

"I'll have another spot, if you please," John said.

They had gone so far into the conversation, John, looking at him intently, felt they must go on with it at once. The feeling was there in both of them, terrifying them, and John wanted to go on with the conversation. "It's Isabelle, he said, "I know it's something about Isabelle."

"Of course, I was an old friend of the family," the priest said apologetically.

"So was I."

"I've just got to go on talking. I hardly know what I'm saying at all, but Isabelle's gone all to pieces. It's rotten, because there's nothing left for her now. She knows how it is with her: I mean she knows all about the sense of proportion. Some girls never think of sin. Isabelle has thought all the time about the sin. There's the complete moral prostration . . . you know she'll go on trying to lose her immortal soul. I think she wants to. That's terrible, you know. Don't you see that, John?"

"She'll try to find a way."

"She'll get so low she'll be finally satisfied."

"But it's the two of them together. Fred, and now the way she's going," John said.

"It's worse about her."

"Why does she have to go on like this?" John said, standing up, staring at the priest, suspecting he was deliberately concealing a solution to a problem that had been troubling him a long time. "That's what I want to know." There were no sounds in the house. The only light in the room was one small electric bulb. Outside, on the sidewalk, someone began to shovel the snow, the steel shovel scraping regularly on the asphalt, gratingly. The smell of gas was growing stronger in the room now the windows were closed: the smell of gas escaping as if it had been there and remained faintly in the air.

"Sit down, my boy," the priest said.

"I'm sorry, but what you were saying was exciting me."

"I shouldn't be talking about it at all."

"We both feel a bit the same."

"I daresay," the priest said, looking intently at his fingers spread out on the table, obviously trying not to go on talking. Taking a big white handkerchief from his pocket he began to mop his head, and said suddenly, angrily, "But wasn't I in on it enough? Did she think I couldn't forget Fred's white face, me standing beside him there on the scaffold?"

"I don't know. What do you mean?"

The priest, regarding him mildly, his head on one side, said simply: "Isabelle came to confession to me the other day." On his face the simple expression changed gradually, his forehead was lined and he frowned, shaking his head slowly. "But she must have known I'd know her. Why did she have to come to me?" he said quietly and simply. John hardly spoke, embarrassed because the priest was actually talking about someone's confession and he would be sorry afterward. Suddenly, John said loudly, leaning forward: "You want to know why Isabelle went to confession to you, do you?"

"Eh, eh, what's this? My God, what am I talking about?"

"I'll tell you. She wanted to get hold of you, too. You've got to feel the way it is with her, do y'see?" Tilting back in his chair he began to laugh loudly, foolishly. "That was neat of her, wasn't it? In that way she just took another hold on you. You've felt how it is with her and now you'll never forget it." Trying to stop laughing foolishly he couldn't get a deep breath and only shook his head.

"You think so?"

"Certainly."

"Oh, this is silly. What am I talking about?" Father Mason took another drink from the bottle on the table and stood up slowly. "I ought to be going home at once," he said. The color was going out of his face and, moving in the room, he lurched to one side, reaching out abruptly, holding on to the back of a chair. Momentarily he stood there, annoyed by his lack of balance, and moved with slow dignity toward his hat and coat, tossed over the bed. His face was expressionless; he was concentrating only on his coat and hat. "How is Lillian?" he said, fumbling with his coat.

"Fine, Father."

"That's good. She's a lovely character and ought to be a Catholic."

"I'll tell her."

"Do so. What about you? Oh sure, you're all right. What am I talking about?"

John helped him with his coat and hat and offered to go home with him, knowing how important it was he should appear dignified and no one in the neighborhood see him. If Father Mason ever thought anybody had seen him slightly intoxicated he would be unhappy for weeks, hardly able to sleep for a long time. So John took hold of him by the arm and they walked downstairs together. It was harder walking outside because the snow was packed down tightly on the sidewalk, and lurching, their feel slipped.

"Am I walking quite all right?" the priest asked.

"Yes, Father."

"You're a good fellow, John."

They had to walk over to the lighted corner to get a taxi-cab, and standing there, holding on to each other's arm tightly, till one came down the street, John felt sympathetic and friendly. He helped Father Mason into the cab and decided to go home with him. He didn't want anyone to notice the priest walking into the house, if he lurched at all.

A light was in the front hall of the priest's house. Arm in arm, they went up the sidewalk, walking firmly and easily, and John left him in the hall, hardly waiting to shake hands, closing the door quickly because Father Mason would be embarrassed, apologizing. It was better to leave him there so he would not have to think of anything before going to bed.

Walking home, John thought of Isabelle, the feeling of resentment growing stronger all the time as he walked faster.

CHAPTER THIRTEEN

*T*he day Lillian came back after the Christmas week John received a letter from Father Mason, a straight-forward simple letter asking him if he would be good enough to write and tell him what had happened after he had started to drink the other night. His mind had been unable to retain a single impression of anything they had said after drinking in the room, though he had a vague feeling he had been in some way ridiculous. He didn't want to be a bother, he said in the letter, but would like it if John would tell whether he had got home in good condition, and if anybody on the street had seen him. The letter had a postscript adding he had resolved never to touch strong liquor again.

John, answering the letter at once, declared they had talked pleasantly in his room, mentioning occasionally Fred Thompson, and he had decided to go home with him, not because he was too unsteady, but there was a possibility he might slip on the sidewalk. And he tried to make it very clear that Father Mason hadn't said anything he need feel ashamed of, and no one had seen him on the street, and it had been easy getting into the house. John avoided mentioning any incident that would have made the priest uneasy, for he liked and admired him and wanted him to have confidence.

It was an effort being good-tempered, writing the letter. On his bed, waking up, he looked for the bedbugs that had bitten him on the chest. His chest was all red from scratching in the night. Before Mrs. Stanley brought him the letter he had been sitting on the side of the bed, wondering how to be assertive without provoking a quarrel and leaving the house. The room was close to downtown, and he felt he would not get another one so cheaply. The notion of spending more money for a room he could not tolerate. It was almost part of the motivating force in his whole plan to remain in the cheap room until ready to do something decisive. So he went down-stairs carrying in his hand the letter he had written to Father Mason, and met with Mrs. Stanley in her kitchen. Bed-bugs were intolerable, he suggested mildly, and was sure it was accidental that they were in the house of such a splendid woman. At first she was outraged, talking rapidly, and he almost forgot why he was standing in the kitchen, looking at her with his mouth open, ready to leave at once. Mrs. Stanley was indignant, thinking he wanted to move away with pay-ing a week's room rent: that was the trouble: and discover-ing he preferred to stay in the house she got into a jolly mood, refusing to take his complaint seriously, as she waved her palm at him. Exasperated, he pulled off his tie, opening his shirt at the throat, showing her the red marks from the bites. For the first time she seemed to understand what he was talking about. "You must have brought them here yourself," she said quickly, then added hastily she would put a steel bed with a new spring in his room, if he would stay.

They shook hands warmly and she waved her palm at him again and he went out of the house, happy and certain he had in some indefinite way saved a lot of money. It was necessary for him to have stability and not move again till really ready.

That evening he was alone with Lillian and held on to her tightly, for he had not seen her all week, and wanted to make love at once. Impatiently he waited while she talked of many things, and the eagerness slowly went out of him. Smiling wistfully, she said fondly, "We do love each other, don't we John?" and then cried a little. He was eager to comfort her, but her thoughts were beyond him, her sorrow was something he did not understand. All evening they were together in the apartment, attentively reassuring each other they were very much in love. Sometimes he talked to her irritably, observing by small gestures her determination to please him. Sometimes she was too serious, ready to talk, and then a little amused at herself. Patiently she sat down beside him and said, "You know what I've been thinking, John?"

"What in God's name has been bothering you?"

"I've been thinking I'm bothered by the feeling I can't help remembering thoughts I had, old thoughts I had before we began to love each other, thoughts of other people." She was talking quietly with so much assurance, he did not contradict her, merely looking at her face, watching her lips moving. "Well, that's a thought you oughtn't to have," he said, "but I don't want it to get stronger. I think I know what you mean, but you be fair while with me, and even when you're alone try and think of me, will you?"

"I think of you all the time, John."

"Not in the right way."

"I know. It bothers me."

She put her arms around him, hugging him and said she honestly believed they could be happy together. Excitedly she talked about a plan for celebrating the new year: they did not want to go to one of the hotels: they were meeting Paul Ross and a girl of his; the four of them were going to a supper dance out at the pavilion by the lake where ice was piled along the shore, and then to a party till dawn.

So on New Year's Eve they went with Paul Ross out to the pavilion by the lakefront. Paul's girl, small and neat, with a bright, cruel face, was named Geraldine, a good-humoredly bawdy girl, shouting all the time she wished she had been born a writer so she could write like Rabelais. Ross was very proud of her and later on, sitting down, eating, he talked to her wittily, prodding her, till she shouted at him, making her voice heard above the clatter of rattles, whistles, and the orchestra, then he smiled at Lillian and John. "That's the kind of girl to have for the evening," he said.

Dancing, they drank and were happy. The piled wine bottles underneath the table. Lillian was so happy she threw her arms around John at midnight when everybody stood up and she kissed him and many women laughed at her.

They left the pavilion to go to the party in the apartment house on one of the streets leading up from the lake, twenty minutes' walk away, and John suggested they walk along the boardwalk, though it was snowing hard, and they were all enthusiastically glad he had thought of it. Earlier in the evening when they entered the dance pavilion, it had not been snowing but was very cold. Now it was snowing, hard thick flakes of snow falling fast and carried away in the strong wind. They were walking along the boardwalk by the lake, past the bleak frames of the stands and the amusement park used only in the summertime, and they heard the lake waves tossing against the breakwater farther out and rolling up to the icy shore. Ice was piled all the way along the shore, down from the boardwalk. Out over the lake it was very black, and passing under one of the streetlights all the snow was slanting in the light, slanting in from the blackness out over the sounding lake. The wind was driving the snow in from the lake and whirling it along the slippery boardwalk, slippery because the snowflakes hardened before hitting the ground. Ice spots on the walk and snow sweeping over, make walking difficult. It felt colder than it had been all winter. They were walking four abreast along the boardwalk, singing a song and trying to make their voices sound loud and important above the sound of the wind, and Lillian impatiently ran on ahead, singing at the top of her voice. John went on walking beside Paul, his chin tucked down in his coat, his hands in his pockets, listening to Geraldine saying she did not like the snow much and wished they had taken a taxi. On ahead, Lillian was still singing, and John suddenly left the others, running on, catching up with her, hoisting her high up on his shoulder, singing with her, then turning around and walking backward, waving to Paul and his girl, who began to run toward them with their heads down. Lillian was sitting contentedly on his shoulder looking out over the lake, hardly talking by the time Paul caught up with them. They went on walking like this a few paces, and she slid down from his shoulder, and walked quietly beside him. Passing under a streetlight he saw that her face was tucked down into the collar of her fur coat.

Suddenly she looked up at him and said, smiling faintly: "It's very fine out here in the wind and snow, isn't it?"

"It's great when we're feeling warm inside from the liquor," he said.

"You know what I'm thinking?"

"No."

"What a pity it is that poor Isabelle is home in bed and sick when she might be out here."

"I thought you had promised not to mention her to me at all. I thought we weren't going to talk about her."

"Oh, don't be a sorehead. It's New Year's Eve."

They had turned up a side street now, walking away from the lake. The apartment house was at the head of the street. It had turned cold so suddenly over night the ice and now had hardened on the branches of the trees and on the corners and walls of the houses. Yesterday's snow had been soft and melting, now it was hard, swirling around their feet, and branches of trees were white to the tips. A policeman, standing on the corner, swinging his arms across his chest to keep warm, looked at them doubtfully as they passed him. His ears looked bit and red. Lillian yelled at him, "Happy New Year, old boy," and he turned suddenly, waving his arms at them as he walked along the street. The policeman began to walk very fast as if in a great hurry, and it was too bad he had no place to go.

John was anxious to get into shelter and express the thoughts that were making him forget the weather. He was irritated because Lillian had talked about Isabelle, and he had decided to tell her about Father Mason and how she had worried him. The wind was driving the snow against his eyes, and his felt hat, pulled down awkwardly over his ears, was all out of shape. They were puffing, the hot breath from the mouths blown over their shoulders.

At the entrance to the apartment house, Paul and Geraldine went ahead on the stair and John said: "Just a minute, you go ahead, I want to speak with Lillian."

"Not here," she said.

"Yes, here."

"What about?"

"I want to speak to you about Isabelle."

"More of your mania again. I'm tired of it."

"No listen." He told her quickly of the evening with Father Mason and how Isabelle had gone to confession and the priest was sure she had deliberately selected him to tell him of the way it was with her, so she would startle and bewilder him. And he told her Father Mason was sickened, certain of her deliberate degradation. They were standing in the lighted vestibule breathing heavily. Snow, melting on John's face, ran in small streams down his neck and under his collar while he wiped his cheek with his glove. He took off his glove quickly and held her hand.

"She simply wanted to go to confession," Lillian said nervously, beginning to pull off her gloves.

"No, maybe yes. But she wanted to go to him."

"No, she's been in bed and sick and thinking of dying and wanted to go to confession. She always was religious."

"Do you know why she wanted to go to him?" he said, holding on to her wrist tightly, almost shaking her, and staring at her.

"No."

"She wanted to draw him into it. He had been a part of it, do you see, and she didn't want him to get away from it as long as she had it to think of."

"No, I tell you, John."

"Yes, we're all a part of it," he said, squeezing her hand, till she winced, pulling it away. "We're all part of it, and we can't get away from it."

Nervously she watched him, the muscles on her face near the corners of her mouth twitching, afraid he had suddenly gone out of his mind, and scared of the uneasiness in her own thoughts. The wind could not reach them in the sheltered doorway, and melting snow fell in drops from their faces. The wind blowing the snow down the street no longer touched them. John, his arm on her shoulder, pulled her toward him, bending over her while drops of water fell from the brim of his had on to her hair and into her eyes.

"She won't let us get away from it," he said.

"I am away from it."

"She's got hold of us. She's got hold of you and me and all of us, and we have to share it with her. I tell you she owns us. She's got possession of us. That's what she wanted. Slowly, in her own way she's taken possession of us."

"I'm away from it."

"No. It's a kind of movement all around us. She's drawn us into it. She's holding us. She won't let us go."

"Stop it, do you hear? I don't want to listen. I want to go upstairs. Let me go. You're crazy."

"No, you've got to listen now."

She said suddenly: "You know what the matter is. You're jealous and a bit crazy. You know how fond I was of Fred Thompson and you know how I love to think of him now."

"You weren't at all in love with him, I tell you."

"You're an idiot," she said, running ahead of him up the stairs to the apartment.

The people in the big room were drinking, talking, and playing a record on a gramophone. John, following Lillian, tried several times to speak to her, but she would not listen, talking always to somebody else. A young man, fat and red-headed, the owner of the apartment, was playing a guitar, stuttering and blushing whenever he started to talk seriously. He had given the guests cushions to sit on and was a little embarrassed, feeling that his party was obviously successful, and proud of its informality. They had to listen to him play the guitar, always standing in the same place in the room, several paces away from the mirror over the mantel and staring, while he played, at his own image in the mirror.

Then Lillian, who was not enjoying herself, trying to avoid John, said she wanted to go home.

In the taxi, John tried to be friendly, and was eager to kiss and pet her. Sitting in a corner, she pushed him away. He said very rapidly:

"Lillian, Lillian, you seem so lonely, Lillian, and I'm far lonelier, sitting here beside you, than I've been when you were miles away. The lines on your face are set and hard. I see it when we pass the streetlights. Smile a little, or even cry, sweetheart. How much better if we were both crying our eyes out, for we're far the unluckiest pair of lovers in the whole wide world. If we could cry together we'd have the one simple sentiment, and it would be so sweet to share any kind of a sharp pain or a sorrow. Just say a few agreeable words softly and easily. Say anything at all, then. I know how you feel about Isabelle, but how often has she called me a prig just when I'm eager for a new simple happiness with you? Lord, if only I could never hear her name again, or never see her image in my thoughts. I'll believe, as you think, that she's perfect, generous, forlorn, and yet lovely, but if only we could walk in different worlds wide apart . . . Look, Lillian, look out the window and see how light it's getting over the housetops in the east; look down the street when the car turns a corner, and still I can see one faint star and the streetlamps are still lit!"

"Please stop talking."

"But if you'd only listen without having any complicated feelings."

"I said before I thought you were jealous of Fred. He's dead, but in a way he seems to grow stronger, and though he was your friend you hate to think of him. Leave me alone. Please stop moving beside me. Sit still. All the words come easily to you and inside you're in a frenzy. I'm tired. I want to go to bed."

At her apartment house he opened the vestibule door, standing to one side to let her enter.

"Good night," she said.

"Am I not coming up?"

"No, good night."

"But I want to come up. I looked forward to it all evening."

"I don't want to have to think of you at all, you bother me. I'm going to bed. I don't want to see you at all. You worry me."

Closing the door quickly she ran up the stairs. He did not follow her, simply stood there till her shoes disappeared around the turn on the stairs. Then he walked back to the corner, looking for a taxicab. It was not yet dawn. It would not be dawn for nearly an hour, but the snow was hardly falling, and no stars were out.

Chapter Fourteen

*H*e did not see Lillian all week. When he telephoned her she was polite, though not willing to see him for a few days until sure of herself. Considerately, she explained she was not trying to avoid him.

At one time his small contribution had been necessary for the maintenance of the apartment, but for three weeks she had been independent of him, earning money of her own from pupils studying the piano.

Now, when she would not see him, he wished he was still giving her money, though he had become niggardly, but they might at least have been held together by the common payments. And then he felt more confident, really believing it would be necessary for her to go on thinking of him, his image becoming so strong in her thoughts she would be tormented until she actually saw him. It had always been that way with him, when she had gone away for a week. He had been so eager to see her he had hoped she would never go away again. This feeling was always so steady and strong in him, he was certain she, too, would feel the force of it, and in a few days would anxiously wait for him to come to her. At first, for days, she would hold aloof, and then begin to think of it as a period of waiting for him. And so confident was he now he began to concern himself mainly with the unimportant details of his life in the rooming house. Mrs. Stanley had not given him a new steel bed yet, but had changed the bedclothes, and made the bed for him in the morning and tidied his room, though he was supposed to do it himself. The room looked so clean after she tidied it in the morning he was too embarrassed to mention the bed to her again. Mrs. Stanley, cheerfully polite, said he ought to understand she was looking for a bargain and expected to have a good new bed in a few days.

Early in the evening he was lonesome in spite of his confidence and self-assurance, and got into the habit of walking north along the streets near Lillian's place, never actually admitting he might possibly see her on the street and have a casual conversation. The second evening he walked north he went closer to the apartment, walking more slowly, for the night was fine, hardly cold, the first days of the January thaw, with plenty of sunlight and snow melting from the roofs of houses and bare spots showing in the lawns and all over the parks. The third time he went even closer to the apartment house, in the late afternoon, and after passing it stood in the doorway of the tobacco shop on the corner, looking back along the street at the house. It was nearly five o'clock in the afternoon, but like the beginning of winter twilight and lights were in the windows of the new apartment house, facing the vacant lots. On the street the lights were not lit.

Standing there smoking a cigarette, mechanically watching a streetcar stop and people getting out and walk along the street toward the apartment-house, he was still hoping to see Lillian, yet nervously aware he would not be able to conceal that he had come there purposely to see her. Three men and a woman who had got off the car where walking briskly along the street, and he followed them with his eyes till suddenly he recognized the woman. Isabelle Thompson had got off the car and was walking along the street to the apartment house.

On impulse he followed her down the street, almost catching up with her, then hesitating, he turned, walking back to the corner slowly, feeling alert and cunning and hoping she had not seen him. Isabelle, who had been sick, was now going to see Lillian, and he thought he might stand on the corner and make a plan that would surprise both of them and have him appear suddenly important, impressive. He was annoyed, leaning against the tobacconist's window unable to think of anything that would help him. He had hurried back to the store entrance, turning, facing the street again, ready to start thinking energetically, and then he couldn't organize his thoughts. Excitedly he kept beating his toes on the sidewalk, ready to run down the street and follow Isabelle into the apartment house, yet assuring himself he was cool and in control. Lights were in the tobacconist's windows, and he looked at the cigars and tins of pipe tobacco.

Still angry, he stood there, no longer trying to think, only he wouldn't walk away from the street corner. Twenty minutes later Lillian and Isabelle, coming out of the apartment, walked toward the corner. Lillian had on a new caracul coat, the skin clipped tight. Isabelle was wearing her heavy dark blue cloth coat. The two girls were walking slowly, arm in arm, Isabelle, a little taller, walking near the curb. John, seeing them coming toward him, was alert and cunning again, all his thoughts clear, so instead of walking down the street to meet them, he hid far back in the store entrance, ready to follow, and possibly meet them casually. It was the beginning of the plan he had started to make in the first place.

They turned at the corner and he followed on the other side, hoping they were going into a store, or even to a restaurant to have afternoon tea. They were not going out for the evening; it was too early and they did not wait for a street-car; besides, Lillian knew hardly anyone in the neighborhood. It was a mild winter evening for a walk, the slush thick by the curb, and autos passing sometimes sprayed the slush over the sidewalk and people shouted angrily at the drivers.

The two girls were merely going for a walk in the late afternoon. Three blocks south they stopped, talked together and turned along the side street running down to the ravine. All these side streets, like the one where Lillian lived, led down to the ravine, but this one led to the cemetery. John, noticing they were walking down to the cemetery where they had buried Fred Thompson, got so excited the careful thoughts went out of his head and he started to walk fast, trying to catch up with them. He had let them get too far ahead, and it was suddenly very important to him that Lillian should not go walking into the cemetery with Isabelle. Hurrying, he whis-tled, but they did not hear him nor turn around. By running he might have caught them, before passing through the gate, but other people walking along the street were watching him and he was confused.

The wide gate between the two stone pillars was still open. Three women in black were coming out of the cemetery. The girls in the brown caracul and blue-cloth coats passed through the gate, turning to the left, out of sight.

Then he started to run, though now they had passed through the gate he did not want to catch up or speak to them; he was eager to follow, curious to know what they intended to do.

Standing by the brown hedge curving along the cinder path leading down the slope, he was out of sight of the girls, yet he could follow them with his eyes. They were walking down to the edge of the cleared land by the row of trees, to the Thompson plot among the new graves on the hill. The snow on the cinder path was slushy and their small shoes had sunk far down. The footprints were there by the hedge. Small streams of water were running by the side of the cinder path, trickling steadily, rivulets running all the way down the path, over the hill and down the ravine. It was very quiet there in the cemetery, all down the hill the sound of running water, trickling away.

The two girls stood together by the heavy stone, hardly moving. They were talking very quietly and John was too far away to hear. Then he saw Isabelle take out a handkerchief and daub her eyes and Lillian began to cry a little, too. It was only an early winter twilight, but with the tall dark trees and woods behind it was hard to follow their movements. In the twilight all the big stones seemed to get larger, and yet were all a part with the snow-covered ground. Then, in the trees below on the hill, a bird cried out and another bird answered and they called to each other, and then a flock of small dark sparrows flew out from the trees across the gray sky to a patch of trees on the other side of the cemetery. Isabelle, kneeling, her coat under her knees, began to pray with her head low, and Lillian knelt down beside her. They put their arms around each other.

Still standing by the hedge, John, glancing at the ground, saw the thick wet snow and was suddenly angry seeing them kneeling there. He was angry and at the same time saddened, no longer caring whether they saw him, so coming from behind the hedge he walked slowly down the path. It was getting dark and soon the caretaker would come and say he wanted to close the gates. The snow melted and water trickled down over the hill, and Lillian kneeling there, looking over the trees and hearing falling water, was praying for a lover in the gray light on the ground where her dead lover lay. She was praying for a lover, and all the time in the light of her own thoughts he was becoming more than he had ever been to her.

John, so close now he could have spoken softly and they would have heard him, felt utterly unimportant and hurt to think he had become insignificant to Lillian and undesired, remembering the feeling from the strong excitement of their love for each other. He was calm now, in the silent cemetery, and he had been so far away they had moved like two figures belonging to the field of snow and mounds and stones. Hardly seeing Isabelle, he knew she was there. Close to her now, all his resentment came back and he trembled a little. He stood beside them and said: "Lillian, please come home."

They looked at him, and Isabelle, blessing herself, stood up. Lillian stood up, staring all around, hardly believing anyone had spoken. Isabelle said quietly: "You startled us, John."

He said quickly: "Don't you think this is about enough, Isabelle?"

"I don't see that it is so surprising."

"You two coming in here now."

"No, people were coming out just when we were coming in. We were out for a walk and thought of coming down here. After all, they close the gates when they don't want us to come in."

She spoke calmly, with assurance. Her cheeks were absolutely colorless but her eyes were bright and a little feverish. The wet snow had dampened all the lower part of her coat and she was coughing.

"Let's walk up out of here," he said, taking Lillian's arm.

Walking beside him, Lillian did not talk at all. The man at the gate, beckoning to them, said he wanted to close for the evening. The gray light remained in the sky and there was a clear outline of a pale moon.

"You seemed to think it peculiar we should come down here," Isabelle said.

"I think it peculiar you should bring Lillian here."

"For my part," she said, "I've been sick, I've had the flu; I've still got it, I guess. I don't know what I've got. But I was thinking of Fred and thought it would be good to go walking with Lillian, and we decided to say a few prayers. Lillian wanted to come, too."

"She didn't."

"I did," Lillian said.

"I think it only natural," Isabelle said, "that a girl should occasionally go to the grave of a man she had loved and think of him. Lillian loved Fred and I loved him." She was talking sensibly without any passion, as they walked slowly through the gates. The lights were now lit on the street.

"Please, Lillian," he said, "tell her she's a fool and a little mad for bringing you down there in the dampness and the water running all down the hill."

"You know I loved Fred," she said slowly.

"But you don't have to be stupid enough to go on thinking about him, though you never did before. You didn't use to think of him."

"But I can't help thinking of him now," she said, and started to cry.

"Do you see?" Isabelle said, looking directly at him.

"I see all right. I loathe you. I hope you're damned. You're beyond redemption. I despise you."

"Stop it, John," Lillian said.

"Don't cry here on the street," he said savagely.

"I can't help it."

"Stop it, do you hear, you little fool."

"You're only making me feel worse."

Turning suddenly to Isabelle he said: "You're to blame for this, you morbid, silly creature. I hate to say anything to make you feel bad, but the trouble with you is you're so egotistical you can't think of anything but yourself. You've got to stop bothering us or I'll wring your neck, do you hear? I'll wring your crow's neck. After tonight go and pick the bones of someone else."

"I think you're a little unbalanced. You misinterpret everything," Isabelle said.

"Don't worry. I've got it right."

"Poor John."

"I'm warning you to leave the two of us alone after tonight."

"Please go home, John, and leave us alone now," Lillian said.

"I'll go. But I'm going to see you tomorrow."

"Please go along now. Go on."

"I'm going."

He walked on ahead of them up the street and turned the corner without looking back.

Chapter Fifteen

*A*t lunchtime, he went to see Lillian, sure she would be in her apartment. All night he had hardly slept, falling asleep a little before dawn, after hearing faintly wheels of the first wagons grinding on the hard snow on the road.

He rapped on the door. Lillian did not answer for a long time. Finally, the door opened, she stared at him and did not ask him to come in. Her eyes were swollen and she was so tired he was all compassion for her and put out his hand, his fingers almost touching her forehead before she drew back quickly: "Please don't touch me," she said.

"Dear, Lillian."

"What do you want?"

"Just to see how you are." He tried to step into the room and she partly closed the door, holding him back, her face sullen and resentful. The edge of the door touching, though not hurting him, irritated him, so he pushed hard, forcing it back, while she pressed all her weight on the other side. They did not speak, just pushed hard against each other as though it were the one important thing to be done at the time. They were both acting foolishly, and he heard her breathing heavily, trying to hold the door as he slowly forced her back, her feet slipping on the hardwood floor.

"This is nonsense," he said.

"Go away, do you hear, or I'll call somebody."

"Don't be a little idiot," he said.

Reaching out quickly, letting the door go, she swung her small hand, slapping him across the face. The door swung wide open, and standing before him, waving her head from side to side, talking rapidly, she said: "You come up here, do you? Of all the gall, of all the gall. And the way you went on talking to me all the time about Isabelle. Leaving the Errington place because it was cheaper. Oh, yes, why not? What else did you do? Of course you had to stop singing in the choir; for what reason was it? Let me see, I forget, let me think. Oh, yes, you were the victim of your environment; wasn't it something like that? Nasty people of low reputation insisted upon being seen in your company. But you could go on hating, couldn't you, couldn't you? You did that best of all and had the strongest hates in the world till you were completely obsessed, and I . . . Oh, yes, that's it, you loved me so much because you hated Isabelle so much. You had to keep it balanced, you . . ."

"Tell me, please tell me, who have you been talking to?"

"Who?"

"Yes, who?"

"Why, Isabelle, of course." Her pale lips moved and trembled, holding them with her teeth.

"Isabelle told you about the Erringtons? Why did she do that?"

"I don't know. She had some decency left and owed something to me. She couldn't see me fooling myself about you, I guess. Oh, go away, why do I have to stand here talking about it to you?"

Instead of answering he smiled at her, his lips drawn too far back, his gums showing, and he held the smile long after the feeling provoking it had passed, and it remained on his face like an ugly grin. He was looking at her, shaking his head jerkily, till finally he spun halfway round, looking at her again, only this time his face was expressionless. Turning, he ran along the hall, downstairs and out the front door.

The air cooled him and he walked along soberly, hardly nervous at all, the surprise gone and no excitement remaining from the conversation with Lillian. His thoughts had really gone far beyond the conversation until it was something he could look back upon as being almost inevitable. The calmness came to him so quickly it seemed to happen almost at once. Across the road a Chinese laundry-boy was getting off his bike, going along the sidewalk leading to the house. When John first saw the boy, carrying the big blue bag, he was still puzzled and excited by the conversation with Lillian and his palms were sweating: then, by the time he looked again at the Chinese boy, his palms were dry: Lillian's feeling seemed inevitable and the event far away: he was hardly thinking of her, just getting ready to steadily rid himself of the source of all his unhappiness. He wasn't even thinking of going to see Isabelle: it had become suddenly necessary to think of her as someone out of his life altogether and out of the life of everyone around him. As soon as this notion began to have an immediate reality for him, he experienced a calmness he had not known for a long time. Putting her far away, and getting rid of her entirely, was such a quick, satisfactory, mental achievement he had a sudden pleasure and was eager to forget everything, walking along the dry spots on the sidewalk, keeping to the outside, near the curb.

But all afternoon and in the evening he was sorry for himself, and had no energy to talk to anybody. His head was tired and aching and lying down he tried to sleep. Though

his eyes were heavy he could not sleep. An unexpected iner-
tia had left him so helpless he could only lie on the bed and
feel sorry for himself. Sitting at the window before lying down
he had tried to hold a hot strong feeling of hatred in spite of
the ache in his head, but it went out of him, and lacking
energy, he lay down on the bed.

After dark, when he could hardly see in the room by the
pale light from the street, he got up and went to the head of
the stairs to ask Mrs. Stanley if she would sell him a cup of
tea and maybe a little bread and jam. She was glad to please
him, she said, for he was never any trouble to her at all. So
she brought the food to him, and standing at the door, her
hands on her hips, and smiling, showing all the roots of her
teeth, said: "It'll be fine for you from now on. A new bed'll
be here in the morning. Isn't that elegant?"

"It's very good of you."

"A nice, new, fresh, bed. What's the matter with you,
aren't you feeling good?"

"I've got a headache."

"You've been eating too much."

"No, I've been thinking too much."

"Well, goodness knows, I'm doing everything I can to
make you comfortable."

He ate the bread and jam, read a few pages of a magazine,
something about neurology in the Arts and Science department of *The American Mercury,* but tiring and wanting something light and easy, he read the editorial, and then yesterday's
newspaper, till he dozed on the bed. Later on Gibbons rapped
lightly on the door and came into the room. John, nearly
asleep, shook his head, indicating he did not want to have a
conversation.

In the morning, when he was sitting in his pajamas, staring at the ceiling, Mrs. Stanley gave him a letter. From Lillian. All the lassitude went out of him as soon as he put the sheets of paper on the table and recognized the writing. The letter said: "Yesterday I talked like a little hoyden, if I remember, but I don't want you to keep having such a thought of me. I was excited and had hardly slept at all, and then you appeared and it was almost more than I could endure. I told you Isabelle had explained to me that she had gone to your place, when you were at Errington's. Don't think for a minute she was pretending you induced her to go there. I believe she tells the truth, saying she went there, first of all, of her own accord. Nor did she try and excuse herself. Nor do I excuse her. She was egotistical, a little spiteful, and on that occasion without much principle, but if you remember she has been that way ever since school days, I am not blind to her faults. She has many faults, but is at least capable of quick, fine feeling. When we were at home last night after leaving you, and feeling close together, she told me of the evening with you at the Erringtons'. I was upset because I was thinking of Fred and at the same time was thinking of you. I really did love you so much, and I was explaining my own confusion to her, trying to find out for myself why I did not think of you as much as I used to. We were talking about Fred, and how he had loved me in the days when you and Isabelle were going together, probably thinking of getting married. Isabelle began to talk to me about you and her old feeling, and blaming herself a great deal, told me of the night she had gone to see you. I felt very sorry for her, though sufficiently indignant to resent even having her there with me, as much as I resented you coming to see me yesterday.

I don't want to see Isabelle again. I told her so this morning, but she is in bed, a relapse of some kind, and a high temperature. She oughtn't to have come out yesterday, thinking she was feeling a little better, to get more of a cold. Anyway, it is over, and so much the better. At one time I was thinking always of Fred and now I can go on remembering him. I shouldn't have tried to love someone so soon after Fred's death when the manner of his murder is still so vivid in my mind. I forgive you for being a little bit mistaken about your feeling for me. We were all mixed up, it seems, and I'm going away to the country for a while."

John read the letter twice, jumped up, tore it in pieces, and threw it at the closed window. He began to dress rapidly. Carrying his overcoat in his arm he rushed out looking for a taxi to go and see Lillian.

But at the apartment no one answered the door and he rapped, listening earnestly, hearing no movement inside, and was satisfied she was not there. Downstairs he asked the janitor if she had gone, and he said she still retained the apartment but had said she was going away to the country and would not be back until spring.

John felt helpless listening to the janitor, because there was not way for him to test his strength. Walking home, he was at first alert, realizing he had seen accurately that Isabelle was taking possession of his whole life and the life of Lillian, and he now could not longer move because she had hold of him, and he was helpless. Excited, he was immensely satisfied that he had seen it all so clearly. Lillian was gone. John had love Lillian and she was always a part of any plan he made for the future, and it was always important that he should be able to tell her about his success. There was no one else to talk to. It was hardly worthwhile being successful unless she could appreciate it. Part of the satisfaction was in the enjoyment of her strong interest. But she was gone out of the city. So he walked rapidly until exhausted. His head felt feverish. He was still strong, but exasperated because he could not use his strength.

CHAPTER SIXTEEN

*L*ying in bed in the morning, all his body became suddenly alert, his arms trembling a little and a fire in his
head. His forehead had a weight pressing against it, and rubbing his hand across it, he felt beads of moisture and con-
templated the shining tips of his fingers. On the bed he sat
up, holding his head, rubbing the temples slowly to drive
away the hotness and the fever so he could think of the idea
coolly. Still he was trembling a little from the first excitement
of the notion and refused to go on thinking. The eagerness
and excitement was there because he clearly saw himself
committing a violent act, but he refused to go on thinking
of the act alone for it was necessary for him to get beyond
the first feeling and see himself critically as an instrument
and was now sure, walking the length of the room, glancing out the window, he had become detached from the normal emotions of resentment and anger. There were hardly any
noises on this street, and a new peacefulness and quiet satisfaction came to him after finding the solution to a problem
bothering him a long time. When Lillian had slapped him
the other day John had nearly approached the solution, but
something seen on the street had turned it away from him.
Even now he wasn't quite ready, for his head was still hot,
his arms trembling and weak.

In this small room at the moment John felt more important than ever before, and suddenly saw himself in a new

relation with all the life around him, and a little beyond it. His own safety in society was unimportant, because nothing anyone did to him could really affect his own unassailable confidence.

He liked to think of himself as a cool, reasonable man, who never found it necessary to move hurriedly, so looking at himself in the glass, feeling the slight growth of beard, he smiled, pleased by his calmness. It was, first of all, with him a matter of strong emotion but just as essentially an ethical matter, for he was an educated man who had been taught for years that passions should be governed by reason: one ought to consider, then have a judgment and a conclusion, just as they used to in college in the first classes in logic. In this way of being reasonable he was different from the man in the street, who having a sudden notion and strong passion, always acted blindly. The only trouble was, John occasionally trembled and his head got hot, though certain now he would not do anything till absolutely calm. It occurred to him to go downstairs and have a talk with Mrs. Stanley, a rather commonplace woman somewhat the same as "the man on the street," and merely measure the strength of her emotions by her opinion of the necessity of sometimes destroying a person. At the same time John was further assuring himself he wasn't in a hurry and quite calm. So he walked out of the room and downstairs looking in the kitchen for Mrs. Stanley, who was sitting at the end of the table, darning a black stocking and crooning a song. Her iron-gray hair was hanging down untidily, dropping over her forehead whenever she leaned forward. There was no music in the crooning song. When she smiled, looking up at him, showing lines of toothless gums, she said:

"What are you excited about, Mr. Hughes?"

"I'm not excited."

"You're pale and kind of feverish-looking."

"I say I'm not excited. My dear lady, I am feeling so calm and well disposed about everything. I came down to talk a few minutes with you." Sitting down beside her he watched her darning the stocking. Her long fingers were swollen at the knuckles from continual attacks of rheumatism. Her face was blotched with dark-brown spots from liver trouble and the same dark spots were on the back of her hands. She was chuckling, grinning, and entirely satisfied with herself. The only think at the moment bothering her was the long strand of hair she could not prevent from falling down over her eyes.

"I only wanted to talk generally, Mrs. Stanley," he said. "It's curious the thoughts continually running through a man's head. You know what I was thinking about up there in my room? You'll never believe it. I was wondering if a man was ever entitled to take the life of another man who was a leech on society, sucking the blood out of people. I suppose it sounds foolish to you, doesn't it? It's an idle thought. It's a bit silly, but what do you think about it?"

"Well, they do do it, don't they?"

"Who does it?"

"They do it at the jail. They takes them out and hangs them and that's all there is to it. Some of them hardly deserve it because they hardly knows what they did, if you see what I mean." Leaning toward him, sticking the needle in the ball of wool, she said: "We all see it differently." Her lower jaw moved jerkily and she was hardly looking at him. "There was my second husband that left me about twenty-five years ago for a trollop he got from God knows where, and went off into another country. I haven't heard of them for twenty-two years and I've got along all right by myself. I've forgotten about them, do ya understand, do ya understand that? I've forgotten about them, but sometimes I wake up at night thinking hard about the slut I never saw. You now what I feel? I feel I'd know her if I ever saw her. I'm quite sure of that. I just have that feeling, lying awake at night and the light from the window falling across my bed. Then I'd know her and I'd reach out and take hold of her with these hands. See them? I'd take hold of her by the windpipe and wring her neck though every tooth had fallen out of her head and she was scarred all over from the pox. Then I'd feel fine, and wouldn't think about her at all afterward. But it was always a steady feeling. I never flew into a rage about it. I just had the steady sensible feeling I'd know what to do. But get along with you, what are you joshing me about, getting me to tattle about things I've felt, and you sitting there with a frozen face?"

"No you ought to go on talking."

"You're joshing me, taking me too much for a simple soul; but I'll tell you, you're just a bit simple yourself, that's why you got me talking to you." She started to laugh and kept on cackling, her face turned up to him, her eyes squinting, then rolling a little from side to side. "Where are you going?" she said quickly. "I thought you wanted to talk to me."

"I'll be back later," he said, turning at the door, hurrying upstairs to get his coat and hat, and feeling immensely satisfied thinking his own feeling wasn't at all strange. The only difference was in his judicial attitude, submitting the feeling first of all to his own good judgment.

Hungry, he went out for a walk downtown to have a good meal that would satisfy him for the whole evening. It was late afternoon and the downtown streets were slushy and the sidewalks wet and steaming near the base of the big stores. John was crossing the street, at the corner of the department store, looking at the plate-glass windows of Childs' on the other side of the road, hardly thinking of anything. Suddenly he stopped, noticing a policeman waving a mitted hand at him angrily, telling him to stay at the curb and wait for the traffic signal. The policeman stared at the stocky man, who had his hands in his pockets and a puzzled expression on his face. When the policeman waved at him John was so startled he did not turn back at once, just gaped at him, his mouth hanging open a little, and hearing the policeman shouting at him, he turned quickly, jumping back to the curb, more excited than he had been all morning. Looking a the big policeman had reminded him of his neglect to provide for his own safety in any of his plans. Until the big man in blue had waved at him, he had never even thought of his own security. When the traffic signal permitted, the crowd crossed the road, and John waited till many were ahead so he would not be noticed.

Such a small precaution as hiding in the crowd annoyed him, for he had the feeling he was enormously more important than anyone crossing the road and wanted to walk out ahead. Instead, he had waited and had passed the policeman uneasily. No one in the crowd noticed him, just a stocky fellow, walking rather erectly, leaning back on his heels, crossing the road slowly.

John had been hungry, but in the restaurant having hardly any appetite at all he would have gone out at once, only it had become a part of his policy to remain calm and normal.

Slowly he ate scrambled eggs and toast and drank two cups of coffee, though it had no taste for him. The restaurant was not crowded in the afternoon, but he was conspicuous, sitting alone at the hard white table, many people passing on the street on the other side of the window. Moving with deliberate slowness he paid his check and went out.

Early in the evening Paul Ross came to see him and found him lying on the bed, his body inert and his eyes wide open. Usually John was glad to see Ross and welcomed him effusively; now, without getting up, he half-heartedly asked him to sit down. "You don't look so good," Paul said. "Isn't it funny I didn't think you'd be feeling so good, so I brought us a drink." He took a quart bottle of whiskey from his pocket. "What's the matter with you?" he said. "Don't you want me to stay?"

"Yes, sit down."

"Get up yourself then."

John, getting up slowly, smiled amiably at Paul, putting an arm around his shoulder. "You're a splendid fellow," he said. "I don't know anyone I like better than you."

"I've always had the same opinion of me," Paul said.

"Did you have a good week?"

"All right. I'm getting sick of working the old soldier stuff. I mean I'm getting sick of the way I have to work it, making it sound such a grand business." He put his elbows on the table, looking down sullenly. His lips moved, sneering at the table, and he hardly heard John talking to him. "What's that?" he said.

"Will I ask Gibbons to come in and have a drink with us?"

"Sure, we'll kid him along. We're both old soldiers, only it made him a revolutionary with a sour stomach and me a magazine salesman. Wait a minute before you speak to Gibbons. I went over to see Isabelle Thompson this afternoon. I didn't know she was sick. She's pretty bad. I couldn't see her. The doctor was there. I like her and often think of her."

"She's worse, eh? Well, she's more effective when she's sick."

"What do you mean?"

"Nothing."

"Stop muttering then; speak out. Isabelle said to me she wasn't interested in living, but she'd hate to die. She'll die hard, hanging on till there's nothing left to give up."

"So much the better then."

"What's that? You sound silly to me. I don't know what you're talking about. You'd better get Gibbons."

John, from the hall, called Gibbons, asking him to come into the room and talk with them. Gibbons was tired and dejected. "I don't feel much like conversation," he said, "but I'll come anyway." The three of them sat around the table. Paul said to Gibbons: "What's bothering you?" "Nothing," Gibbons said. Though reticent naturally, and a revolutionist, having no respect for sentimentality, he was anxious to talk to somebody. Slowly and earnestly he explained he was feeling bad because he was going to lose his job as an organizer for the party. They were willing to let him go on organizing, but he wouldn't get any salary for it. The party wasn't doing very well and they were cutting down expenses. Some of the organizers had to be dropped from the salary list, and since he had disagreed with the executive, a dispute over left-wing and right-wing communism, he was going to be dropped from the list. It was mean in a way, he said, since it was his money that had started the party in the country: he had even sold his furniture to help them along. He was speaking quietly, anxious for their sympathy, and trying to conceal his own feeling, determined to express a good revolutionary spirit.

"Drop them," Paul said.

"Oh, no, I'll go on organizing. I think my sympathy for Trotsky had something to do with it. I advocated what we call Trotskyism because I can't help thinking he's a great man. He's the biggest man in the movement. It wasn't so much that I wanted the comrades to agree with me; I merely thought something ought to be said for Trotsky."

"Have a drink now."

"No, I don't touch it at all, but you fellows go ahead."

They talked to Gibbons as though anxious to rid him of his oppressors, he was such a nice fellow. They both had a drink, and John said to Gibbons: "Doesn't it make you feel that you'll kill somebody?"

"Oh, no."

"Don't you ever feel that way?"

"No, I try to be dispassionate about it."

"You know, Gibbons, it's a thing John can't help talking about. You were at the war and saw it was different, didn't you?"

"I know," Gibbons said. "But I don't believe in capital punishment, for example, but I do think the lives of a few individuals are unimportant when the good of society is involved."

Paul, who had been drinking too rapidly, examined the bottom of his empty glass, and said: "Of course, the first time you knew you actually had killed someone it was a little different than simply firing away, not knowing who you were hitting. It reminds me of the time Fred Thompson had to stand close to someone for the first time and shoot him. Fred was a lieutenant in charge of a party that had taken some prisoners. A few Germans were lying there dead and wounded in a big jagged hole. We were all standing there resting, surprised at the size of the shell hole. One of the Germans, who had been knocked down and badly wounded, an old gray-haired square-headed man over fifty, got up suddenly, and swaying and grabbing his rifle, fired at some of us. He was only a few feet away and didn't hit anybody, because he could hardly hold the gun at his shoulder. He was an old fellow with a puzzled, stupid, bewildered expression on his face, who had gone a little crazy, and kept swinging his head, trying to fire. He was apt to hit someone, too. The men all stood there looking at Fred, who was the officer in charge, instead of taking a shot at the old fellow. Fred looked at the old German, hesitated, and pulling out his revolver shot him through the side of the head. The bewildered expression never went off the fellow's face. Fred looked at the man lying there dead and looked at his own men, and felt sick. He did not know what he ought to have done, but the men were so disgusted they turned their backs on him. Some of them wouldn't speak to him for days. It was just a cold execution by an inexperienced officer who had nothing against the poor old fellow."

"That was bad. There was not excuse for it," John said.

"But Fred didn't know what to do, and the men were looking at him."

"What would you have done?" John said.

"Just about the same. There are no heroes; some get medals, some don't. I would have wanted to do the right thing and would have done what he did."

Paul, who had been drinking too rapidly, took another one quickly, looking at the color of it against the electric light. "I smell gas in here," he said.

"It's always here."

"It's not a good smell."

Fumbling in his inside pocket he brought out two small medals with bits of colored ribbon attached and tossed them on the table. "I make them work for me, but I'm through with them now," he said. The medals made a small sharp sound on the table. Paul, looking at them, smiled, and waved his arm in a wide circle. His eyes were bright, his arms still waving, and his lips were drawn back, though he hadn't said anything. "Fred oughtn't to have done that," he said, and crouching down in the middle of the floor, his eyes staring, mumbled: "The trench is a gash, a wound. I can't run, I can't run, I got to stay here. I can't run. They're coming, but I can't see them and I can't run." He moved slowly toward Gibbons, who backed away from him to the other side of the table. Paul, straightening up suddenly, stood stiffly, his mouth open, staring at the bright light, then lurched toward Gibbons, swearing, muttering, and sure he had to kill him.

John and Gibbons held him, pushing him slowly toward the bed. They held onto him while he breathed heavily, his eyes blinking, looking vaguely at both of them, shaking his head slowly, smiling stupidly.

"He'll probably go to sleep now," John said, walking away from him. Gibbons sat on the bed beside him, and finally said: "I think I'll go now."

"All right."

Gibbons went out. John looked out the window, down the street as far as the cathedral. The base of the cathedral was dark and wide and heavy, all shadowed, but the silvered steeple shone in the moonlight and the illuminated cross was bright. The talk of the war had made John uneasy and taken some confidence out of him. He was afraid of his own thoughts, though assuring himself he was simply standing at the window waiting to feel strong again. Looking out, he felt vaguely that something would occur, so it would not be necessary to go on with his plan, and he was weaker than he had been all day. Then, looking at the base of the cathedral, he thought it would be quite reasonable to go over there, inside the church. People still hurrying up the walk to the door. It was something to do at the moment and it wasn't necessary to feel he was trying to resist the strong emotion making him go on with his plan.

Before going out the door he glanced at Paul Ross, who was dozing lightly.

CHAPTER SEVENTEEN

*D*ownstairs he opened the front door, standing on the steps and feeling cool air striking his hot forehead. There was no wind, the air was crisp and cool, and on cracks in the steps were thin strips of ice from the snow melting at noontime and frozen now. On the steps he slipped, but held his balance by lurching forward, stumbling along the sidewalk to the lamppost on the street.

The cathedral was across the street and down half a block. A small light was burning at the peak of the Gothic arch and two women went in, closing the door carefully. John, standing by the lamppost, looking across the road, smiled confidently, nodded his head twice and walked over to the cathedral, smiling because he had a splendid notion of a joke in his head. In the shadow of the cathedral he stopped smiling, almost ashamed of himself, and sure he had thought of it as a joke merely because it had humorous possibilities, when really he was going into the cathedral out of fairness, anxious to expose himself in every way to orthodox ethics. In his own room, looking out the window at the cathedral tower, it had occurred to him to cross the road and go to confession, and explain simply that he was ready to kill a woman because it was necessary for his own salvation. Such a notion contributed to his dignity.

Without admitting it, John was anxious to go into the cathedral and talk with someone sensible and steady, so he would forget all about having to go to Isabelle Thompson's house tonight. He wanted something to happen that would prevent him going on with a plan, and yet leave him feeling strong and important.

For years he had never thought himself a Catholic, and unable to feel religious it was nearly ten years since he had gone to confession. Now the cathedral had suggested a whole system of ethics and he had muttered, deceiving himself, that he would offer his own notions in opposition and retain the feeling he had not been in a hurry at all. It was a Saturday night and many people were going to confession in the cathedral. Women sitting on one bench along the wall and men on another one were not interested in each other, bowing their heads, muttering prayers and patiently waiting in turn. It was a large cathedral and only the altar candles and a few lights were lit, so people in the aisles, kneeling before pictures of the Stations of the Cross, were one with the shadows of the pillars and the pews.

John sat down in a pew with three men and a woman who were leaning back reading prayer books. He ought to have knelt down and said a few prayers; instead he tried to feel comfortable, smiling slightly at the man next to him, who nodded formally without looking up. John, a little self-conscious, sitting in the pew, feeling he did not have the same motive as the other people around him, picked up a prayer book out of the rack, attached to the back of the pew ahead, and began to read a preparation for making a good confession. The prayers and interrogations all interested him, and mechanically he began answering questions, getting ready a decent confession, only he never submitted his main plan and purpose to any of these questions. There wasn't any relation between anything he was reading, the list of all the sins, venial and mortal, and the one act he was getting ready to commit. Restive at last, he dropped the prayer book and stepped out of the pew to sit on the penitents' bench beside a handsomely dressed man with manicured fingers folded around fat knees. John was so restive he was sweating, his head hot again, and trembling, ready to rush out and go ahead at once. This feeling, getting the better of his judgment, terrified him, because he had been trying to repress it all day, and it left him cold and dizzy after it had passed away.

He went into the confessional and was alone, the curtain drawn behind him. The panel behind the wire grating was drawn and it was very quiet, but listening intently he heard faintly a woman's voice mumbling on the other side of the confessional. His lips were dry, his heart beating so loudly he could feel it in his throat and thought he would not be able to get his breath. He became calm again, wondering whether he was excited from being in the confessional or from the same emotion that had been exciting him all day. Though calm, wondering about it, he was uncertain, and yet curious about the confessional, as he got ready to hear the panel moving.

Before the panel swung back he heard the priest whispering rapidly, and imagined the woman had finished her confession, and soon the priest, giving her absolution, would be making the sign of the cross over her, praying and blessing her, and reaching with one hand to swing back the panel and incline his ear to the penitent on the other side. Then the panel moved, swinging back, and John was alone with the priest, and trying to see whether he was young or an old man he leaned forward, pressing his nose against the wire. The wire felt cold against the tip of his nose. The priest, waiting patiently, said in an old tired voice: "Yes, my son."

John, moving his lips rapidly to get into the rhythm of a good confession, could not remember the prayers and said simply: "Bless me, Father, for I have sinned."

All the questions he had read in the prayer book were in his mind as he enunciated many small venial sins that could not be expected to interest the old priest, who was leaning back, his hand over his eyes, his elbow resting on a ledge underneath the wire grating.

Then John said finally: "What I want to talk about is this, Father: it's in my mind to kill somebody. It's been in my mind many hours now, but I didn't want to move rashly or just be carried away by a violent passion."

The priest was silent. John, expecting him to lean forward, pressing his face against the wicker, was disappointed when the priest hardly moved his head, an old priest, accustomed to many peculiar penitents. John was offended, sure that he was extraordinarily interesting to anybody who knew some of the thoughts in his head. The priest ought to look at him, startled. He was suddenly angry.

"You did quite right to come to confession," the priest said.

"Yes, Father."

"How long is it, you say, since you were at confession?"

"About ten years."

"Hmm. It's not surprising, is it, that you have such violent thoughts? What do you expect if you never go to communion in a decade?"

"That's not the point, Father. I mean going to communion has nothing whatever to do with it. I'm here now. I felt I wanted to come here and see what you'd say . . ."

"Now don't argue with me."

"But you must understand, I want to listen patiently to you."

"You mean the idea is still in your head?"

"Yes."

"Goodness. You're a strange fellow. Why come to confession if you're not in a penitent mood?"

They were whispering too loudly and the priest stopped suddenly, leaning away from the wire. John was sure he was waiting for time to think. Leaning toward him again the priest said: "The thought is still in your head, is it? All right, then. Have you been drinking at all?"

"Just a glass."

"Yes. But you sound like a sensible fellow. See here now, look at it this way: is there any single emotion in life strong enough to make you want to kill a fellow man? Are you feeling well? Do you really have the thought? In the first place, what has anyone done to you . . . ?"

"She took possession of my whole life. She got hold of all my feelings, trying to own me, and then tried to take everything away from me. She would be better dead."

"A woman, eh? I thought so. That's a little different. It's bad to be carried away by any feeling about a woman. Of course, men want women. God has foreseen it, and so marriage is a sacrament, though not even all marriages are happy, because the principals are human. Outside of that, how often have they been a temptation from time immemorial? And if you, my dear boy, think you are undergoing any kind of a temptation compare it for a moment with the temptations the martyrs endured, glowing with zeal from thinking of Jesus Christ hanging on the cross. Feel how puny and weak your own temptation is. What temptation can you possibly have that hasn't been dwarfed by the temptation of blessed men who died in agony, refusing relief?" The priest was talking rapidly, trying to get hold of a single idea he could use effectively. Pausing, he said eagerly: "You're an educated man, aren't you?"

"I suppose so."

"Of course. Well then you understand something of the dignity of the human spirit. All the nonsense ever written by the wise men of today can't destroy the fundamental dignity of the human spirit. It should be the aim of every Christian to preserve that dignity and be ever watchful of any temptation, which if yielded to, might destroy it. Does that appeal to you?"

"Yes, Father, go on."

"Certainly you can't have any Christian dignity, nor can you have pride in your own spirit, if you are a murderer. The chances are you would never commit such a crime. Still, you have had the thought and it's a sin and that's why I'm talking to you. I'm talking to you as one reasonable man to another. How would you feel afterward? Penitent, of course, and you'd come right back here to me. Even though your crime were never detected, all the years of your life you'd be struggling to make some atonement, always looking for a sedative, something to restore your own feeling of decency and dignity. If you committed such a crime do you know what it would be like? It would be like a bombshell exploding underneath your ego and you would destroy yourself. Your soul would be damned in the next world, but yourself, your ego, that gives you the force to hold up your head, would be destroyed now, I tell you."

"That's it, my ego has been destroyed now, I tell you."

"It has not been destroyed. You're here now, in the arms of the church. The Mother of God will sustain you if you need her. All the strength of the Church and all the goodness she has stored up in heaven for two thousand years is there to support you."

"I can't think that far, Father."

"Have you a feeling of sorrow for letting yourself go this far?"

"No, Father."

"Then what can I do for you?"

"I wanted to be fair."

"You're a decent fellow. Tell me, will you come and see me again? I won't give you absolution now. Don't try and banish that violent feeling: let it come out and then consider it like a reasonable man. Come and see me soon, will you?"

"I'll try to."

The priest began to pray. John's knees on the stool where hurting him. Some of the priest's talk had made his head get hot again. His legs were twitching. Getting up he walked out of the confessional, still hearing the priest praying.

At the pew he got his hat and walked down the aisle. Turning, he saw the priest come out of the confessional, and hesitating look after him, an old priest with white hair holding his head on one side, hardly knowing whether to hurry down the aisle after him or regard it as a conversation with a man whose eagerness for violence had been tempered by good counsel. The priest, watching the short, thick-set man, who was hurrying too rapidly down the aisle, shook his head twice and went back to the confessional, wondering if he ought to have another conversation with a policeman. John felt sorry, for the priest had agreed with him that his own importance had been destroyed. His own soul had been denied to him, but he had a plan that would restore his own feeling of decency and dignity. He had not expected to get such an explanation of the strong feeling from the priest. He swung open the door, stepping out into the cold, exalted, excited, thinking of doing the act that would restore to him all the dignity and decency of the spirit, he, a man of talent, anxious for all the good things, was entitled to.

CHAPTER EIGHTEEN

*N*ow that he was ready, all the resentment he had ever
had for Isabelle was strong inside him. The feeling
was so strong he was a little dizzy, walking along the street,
clenching his fists tightly and slowly relaxing the fingers. It
was not a dizziness making him sway on his feet, only objects
on the street had no meaning for him; the streetlights had fading, many-colored rings of light around them. The air was
cool, but the light breeze simply dried the perspiration and
then his forehead got hotter. For several blocks he walked
rapidly, carrying his hat in his hand. Since he wasn't thinking
of anything at all, just holding the feeling, his legs moved
faster as he breathed jerkily, heavily. Alert, suddenly he
glanced around, wondering if people were noticing him.

The Thompson house was east of the cathedral, on a street
leading down to the park, in an old section of the city with
small houses often freshly painted. The snow was shoveled
from the sidewalks along the street and it was easier walking. The soles of his shoes came down evenly on the cement
walk. Putting his feet down so firmly on the clean cement he
had a long springy stride. The heel and sole, sounding firmly,
gave him more confidence. Hardly anyone was on this street
at ten o'clock. The sound of his own shoes on the pavement
reminded him that he was a solitary man, apart from everybody, and a new exultation exhilarated him till his warm
flesh tingled. The method John had been groping for had

worked itself out so neatly he could hardly believe he had ever had any trouble with it. Isabelle, in bed, would probably be dozing, hardly aware of anyone moving near her, and it would be easy to smother her, and he could have the feeling in his hands. It might turn out to be the same as a death from natural causes.

John intended to go into the house quietly without disturbing anyone, and upstairs to Isabelle's room without being seen. It was important that her mother should be asleep so he would not see her. John was trembling again, his whole body affected by a sudden fever.

The house was only half a block away. Down the street was one park gate leading into the zoo. The sea lion cried out hoarsely. Many people in the neighborhood had protested in the paper the other day against the roaring of the sea lion, urging that the beast have its vocal cords removed.

Slowly he went up the front sidewalk to the veranda, listening carefully. A light was in the hall, one light in the front room upstairs. So far he had walked up to the house like an ordinary man, an old friend of the family, who knew where he was going. None of the excitement inside him affected the way he climbed the veranda steps, a stocky man, a little pale under the light, moving with assurance.

Turning the handle of the door he expected it to open readily, for the Thompson's, an old family in the district, often did not lock the door at night. It was enormously important, suddenly as he turned the handle and stepped into the hall, that he should not see the mother at all.

On tiptoes he climbed the stairs, moving noiselessly on the thick carpet, always found on the stairs in these old houses. The smallest sounds were heard by him. A clock was ticking somewhere downstairs. Someone was breathing heavily in a room at the head of the stairs, and in the upper hall, leaning forward on his toes, listening outside the bedroom door, he was sure it was Mrs. Thompson. All his confidence was restored. His temples began to throb. He could hardly get his breath, trying to draw it in a great gulp and let it out noisily. His whole body was light, every muscle moving easily and feeling strong. Slowly he opened the front room door, shoving his head through the gap and seeing Isabelle lying on the bed, her body stretched out, her head turned to the wall. A small reading lamp was on the table at the head of the bed. She was lying there so calmly he carelessly walked across the floor to the bed.

A few days ago she had look ill, but now, fascinated, he could only stare at her. Her eyes were closed, the lids puffed and swollen, and her lips a brilliant red. Two faint red spots glowed high in the pallor of her thin sunken cheeks and the cheekbones stuck out whitely. There was the hollow and the shadow in her cheek, and the light spot over the bone. Though she was dozing, her thin dry upper lip moved imperceptibly back, showing the dead bluish red of her gums. John could hardly move and only stood there, bending over, and waiting for some of the strong feeling to return and the muscles of his arms and hands to move of their own accord. It was not good hoping to do anything, forcing himself, and he waited for a muscular movement to become part of the thoughts in his head.

Isabelle moved, opening her eyes slowly, staring at him, smiling. "Hello, John," she said. "How did you get in here?"

The uneasiness went out of him hearing her calm voice. Her face and her body had seemed beyond him, but now her calm voice restored all his confidence. Bending over her he took hold of the edge of the bedclothes, ready to pull them up over her head smothering her.

"You look ghastly," she said, still speaking calmly.

"Eh, what's that?" he said, startled to hear her speaking when everything was ready for him.

"You look ghastly. What's the matter?"

"Shut up, do you hear?"

"Where's Mother?"

"In the other room."

"Please don't wake her. We should have had a nurse for me, but we couldn't afford it and she's all tired out now."

Even yet he was sure of himself, smiling at her, thinking he was not going to be disturbed in the house. Holding his hands still only with a steady effort, while he had the necessary satisfaction of telling it to her, he said quietly: "You know what I'm going to do, Isabelle? I'm going to kill you. I'm going to wring your neck. I told you I would. Now I'm going to do it. If you yell, I'll strangle you."

"No."

"I'm going to."

"Don't. I don't want to die."

"You're going to."

"What's the use, John?" she said, trying to get her breath. Twice she tried to speak, still looking at him, but could not get her breath. Still he enjoyed waiting for her to speak, curious to hear the words she would use, hoping to interest him. The effort to breathe was so difficult two faint drops of perspiration appeared on her forehead. They were there, and he saw them on her forehead and then they were gone again.

"God damn you!" he said, working himself up. "This is good for both of us. It's good for you and it's good for me." He put one hand on her throat, pressing her neck down on the pillow. Her neck felt soft and warm. She was muttering: "I don't want to die, John."

"Shut up!" he whispered.

"I'm dying anyway," she said. "Sometime next week. I've got pleura-pneumonia. The doctor says I'll live about a week. He told me and didn't tell Mother."

"Damn you!" he said, shaking her. "You're lying now. You're trying to cheat me. That's it."

"Look at me," she said.

He was looking at a woman who was going to die quickly and was so close to death his own strength, which might have killed her, seemed weak and unimportant beside the slow movement of the force destroying her. His own resolution seemed a little foolish now, looking at her in this way, aloof from her and despising her, and watching her dying. His head, which had been so hot, began to sweat; all his body, held so tensely before, began to relax. His clothes felt heavy, hanging on his shoulders.

"There's no chance?" he said.

"None."

"What happened? You got a cold on top of the flu, eh?"

"Yes."

"Well, I'll go."

"Wait. I don't want to die. But you felt like killing me, didn't you?"

"I did. I really did. I had to. I've got to get rid of you."

"You would have killed me, then they would have caught you and hanged you. They would have put you in the jail down in the corner of the park, in the cell where they put Fred. They put them all there don't they?"

"There's no use talking about it."

"It would be odd, you and Fred dying the same way."

"Stop it, do you hear? Stop."

"A crowd might have gathered around the jail, too. I read about the way they gathered around the jail the night before they hanged Fred. Do you remember?"

"Please stop talking, Isabelle."

"I ought to, but you know you wanted to kill me. Fred didn't want to kill anybody, but you'd both be there. Only you're alive now and he's dead, but you're one together now."

"You're delirious. I'll call your mother."

"No, you'd both be there. So there's the bond between you, the living and the dead. You can't get away from it now."

Helpless, he shuddered, watching her lips trying to move into a smile, and feeling she had hold of him more tightly than ever before, till he was one with her and her brother and all of them, only now he was not longer anxious to get away from it; almost calmly, and with a new, unexpected humility, accepting it.

"I think I'll sit down on the end of the bed," he said.

Isabelle had closed her eyes and was almost asleep. The flushed spots on her cheeks were glowing more brightly, her lips holding the half smile. It was quiet in the room, the faintest noises in the house clearly heard; the ticking of the clock downstairs was distinct.

"You were cruel about it," he said.

Opening her eyes lazily she said: "You were away from me and had become beyond me and wanted to remain beyond me."

"No, I didn't."

"Yes, you were running away from the whole thing. Everybody runs away from it."

"I didn't want to go on thinking about it."

"You were selfish."

"I know. I wanted to get away from it."

"So was I selfish. But I don't want to die now. If only I could go on living."

He said quietly: "Dear Isabelle, why did you have to spoil everything?"

"I didn't want to. Perhaps I always loved you."

"You still love me?"

"I think so, John."

"Lord, Lord, I should have gone on loving you. I don't know. I can't go on thinking any more." Unable to find any more words, he was tired and ready to cry weakly. Isabelle, who had been talking too long, moved restlessly, hardly looking at him. Her eyes, hard, and bright, turned to him no longer seemed to see him. In the next room he heard Mrs. Thompson moving. The old lady came into the room, a black woolen shawl over her shoulder, and offered her hand to John, shaking hands firmly, without smiling.

"I heard someone talking," she said. "It was good of you to come in without waking me. You were always a good boy around here, John."

Looking at Isabelle she moved the bedclothes around her neck, trying to keep from crying. She implied, smiling a little, she was being weak because she was old, though even if Isabelle died she would accept it quietly with confidence in her own strong faith and its superiority over everything she knew about living.

"She's pretty low," Mrs. Thompson said.

"She'd better sleep. I'll go now."

"Come soon again, John."

"I will."

Back home in his room, he got into bed quickly, hardly thinking of anything, he was so tired. Paul Ross had gone. There was satisfaction in being so tired and ready for sleep. After turning out the light he remained awake only a few minutes, making a new pattern out of all the thoughts of the last six months, and then he fell asleep.

CHAPTER NINETEEN

*A*ll the next week John was more contented than he had been all month. Sometimes he thought of trying to find Lillian, but his new notion of her was always stronger. It was better, he thought, to have her go her own way, for between them there would never be any of the calmness he had found for himself now she was sure she had loved Fred, and he knew of the confusion that always would be in her thoughts of him. In the afternoons he went swimming in a Y.M.C.A. tank, paying each time for it. Hardly anyone was in the tank, the kids were at school, and only one gray-haired old man, his skin wrinkled like a roasted apple, sitting at the end of the tank where the sun came through the glass, was always there, his feet dangling in the water. The water looked green and cool and deep in the tiled tank and John swam slowly length after length, following with his eyes on the water the strips of dark tiles wriggling, snakelike at the bottom of the tank, when the surface of the water was disturbed. Sometimes he swam underwater, holding his breath a long time, going the length of the tank and feeling the cool water slipping down his body and over his face. Sometimes he swam for half an hour on his back, dipping his palms in the green water, and kicking his legs infrequently. He rested, sitting under the glass dome at the end of the tank where the sunlight fell on his shoulders. Then he dropped into the green water, swimming easily and contentedly until his shoulders were tired, and then he got out and rubbed himself with a towel till his skin was red and tingling, and talked casually with the old man, who was a good swimmer.

Later in the afternoon he walked over to the Thompsons' and sat for an hour having a cup of tea with the old lady, who was glad to see him. She knew Isabelle was dying and was waiting patiently. She would suffer bitterly, but always there was something to fall back on, for she was a good Catholic and believed that she, too, would soon die, and it would be only a little while before everything would be finally understood, and so sure was she of an inherent goodness in everybody, because of the compassion in her own nature, she thought death was often beautiful. Sitting at the table, a small woman, a little stout, with a smooth face, she asked him about his music and commented on the slow advancement in the city. He told her he intended to go to Maestro Cavalcanti, the most expensive teacher of opera in the city, who was well known in the old countries, and pay him to arrange for a year of training in Italy. It would take every cent he had, but he wanted to try it. Nothing might come of it, but he would always be easier in his own mind. Mrs. Thompson encouraged him.

She never talked about Fred, and hardly even talked about Isabelle.

John saw Isabelle only twice. Once she did not seem to know he was in the room. The second time she held out her hand to him and he kissed it, but they did not talk.

He could not understand why he spent so much time talking to her mother, whose calmness, hopefulness, and superiority over the circumstances of death almost embarrassed him. Mrs. Thompson told him Lillian had written to her, asking about Isabelle, and was coming to the city to see her.

The day Isabelle died Father Mason and John and Lillian and Ed Henley came to the house. Father Mason was almost too cheerful, because he was used to the notion of death, and said to John: "It's the best thing for her. What's there to worry about now? She died quite peacefully, didn't she?"

They had expected her to die, but Ed Henley had never thought about it till now and his eyes were red and he hardly talked to anybody. There was no excitement in it for him, someone he had loved was dead and he couldn't get used to it.

Afterward John and Lillian walked over to the corner together, talking carefully, speaking slowly, both anxious to be polite and friendly and yet reticent. It was a cold day and the wind was blowing up from the lake and chilling them. It was a dark day in the week, when the sun hardly came out at all. After the January thaw the cold days came when the slush on the streets hardened overnight and a cold wind blew steadily. All the signs on the streets were swinging high on the poles and few people came out. Two men holding their hands over their ears went running down the street to a car stop. The snow was falling only thinly. If it had snowed it would have got warmer, but it would not snow all week. The hard cold days of February were ahead.

"These are cold bad days," John said.

"It will last all month," she said.

"Shall we go into Childs' and have a cup of coffee? It will warm us."

"I'd rather not," she said. "I made an appointment at my place for half an hour from now, with some pupils."

"What are you going to do in the city?"

"Go on teaching the piano. I'll get back my pupils and I was doing fairly well. What about you?"

"I'm going away, if I can – if old Cavalcanti can arrange it."

"That's what you ought to do."

"Old Mrs. Thomspon is rather wonderful, don't you think?"

"She has more calmness in the face of life or death than anyone in the city."

"It's funny. Neither Fred nor Isabelle was much like her. They were so excitable."

"Isabelle used to be a little like her."

"She was. In her way she had her own strength and her own pride and had to try and satisfy it, and things got a little mixed up for her."

"She was always very fond of you."

"I've been thinking so."

"She was, I know. She loved you."

"It sounds a bit funny, Lillian, but in a way I must have gone on loving her, only I was always trying to get away from the feeling."

"Well . . ."

"Oh, well . . ."

They were at the corner where the streetcar stopped. The wind was blowing and Lillian was holding her hat on with one hand and her coat down with the other. A car was coming and they went to speak, but the wind carried the words away. It was such a cold wind it was more important Lillian should not miss the car than they should go on talking.

END NOTE

One of life's small ironic satisfactions came to me from this book. When I was writing it in Paris in 1929, the only one I talked to about it was Scott Fitzgerald. The last time I saw him, early one afternoon at the Café Deux Magots, I went over the whole story with him and he was full of questions and lively interest. A few months later we were exchanging insults over my boxing match with Hemingway. Fitzgerald had to make a formal apology to me. Years passed. In the early sixties, reading the *Letters of F. Scott Fitzgerald*, my eyebrows went up. He had written, "If you think Callaghan hasn't completely blown himself up with this deathhouse masterpiece, just wait and see the pieces fall." Then I got a letter from Edmund Wilson, who at the time was in Rome, asking me how it was that the "deathhouse masterpiece" was the one book of mine he hadn't read. When Wilson returned to America he got hold of the book. One night he telephoned me from Talcotville. He said he had been unable to put the book down he liked it so much, and then he told me not to kid myself about Fitzgerald: "Scott would know how good a book that was." Wilson insisted the Fitzgerald comment came out of his emotional involvement with Hemingway after the insults. As everyone knows, Fitzgerald regarded Wilson as his literary conscience. Well, it took some years, about thirty-five in fact, but I was able to say to myself, "Well, there you are, Scott."

MORLEY CALLAGHAN

Norman Snider is a Toronto screenwriter and author. He has written the screenplays for films such as *Dead Ringers, Call Me: The Rise and Fall of Heidi Fleiss,* and *Rated X.* In 2009 he wrote the true crime story *Smokescreen,* which was then adapted for film as *Casino Jack* – it premiered at the Toronto International Film Festival in 2010. To coincide with the release of the film, Exile Editions brought out the complete screenplay, along with storyboards and a director's photo journal, as the first book of its *Exile Silver Screen Series.*

Questions for Discussion and Essays

1. A reviewer said, in 1930, of *It's Never Over*, that the real subject of the novel is the effect of the hanging on the murderer's sister, her emotional disturbance having the effect of "throwing Isabella entirely off her moral balance." If this is true, and it is, could you argue that capital punishment, rather than restoring any kind of balance to society through ideas of justice having been done, retribution and deterrence, must, by its nature, throw that very society, complicit in the death, off its moral balance?

2. That same reviewer observed that one of Callaghan's great distinctions was his avoidance of words like "love" and "hate" and "contempt" and "shame" – seeking rather to describe in the simplest possible terms those emotions that have no names. If this is true, cite several examples of how Callaghan achieves this, of how such moral awareness and complexity is inherent in his direct, straightforward style.

3. In one of his later novels, Callaghan describes a man who, in response to the War and its horrors, determinedly became impersonal, became an amiable, very successful corporate man in the business world, seemingly available to all yet entirely aloof, a master of public relations, a man devoid of any deep personal relations. This man is described by another character as someone who "committed treason against himself..." Can you see the roots of this Callaghan view of human relations in *It's Never Over*, wherein betrayal of the self leads to the conviction that men and women who insist on their own independence, their own personal and very private sense of themselves in public, inevitably become outlaws of a kind? Discuss.

4. Norman Snider says *It's Never Over* is a meditation on sexuality, on possession – in the spirit of Dostoevsky. Discuss the characteristics of this book as a meditation, and what does he mean by "possession?"

5. Snider also says that the sensibility of the novel is essentially Christian and forgiving. What do you think he means by "forgiving" in terms of the characters and the story they live through?

6. As a response to the First Great War, it would be interesting and instructive to compare the effect of *It's Never Over* with a fictional reconstruction of that period, Timothy Findley's *The Wars*, especially since violence in the Callaghan story is implied, the violence is present as a kind of abscess of the spirit, a psychic wound. Discuss.

7. Discuss what might be called the symbolic role of sexually transmitted disease in the novel, disease that is destructive not because it violates puritan standards of sexuality, but disease as it is indicative of a parasite "within."

8. Discuss what Snider means by "a therapeutic sentimentality" that asks for "closure" when confronted by death, and describe how *It's Never Over* "refutes this Wal-Mart optimism."

9. *It's Never Over* takes place against the backdrop of Scots-Presbyterian Toronto society, but the story exists within the Catholic community, which includes the priest. The question is, how large is the role played by religion – in personal terms and institutional terms – in this novel and, if religion does play a part, how orthodox is the role of the priest, how orthodox are his views?

Related Reading

Aaron, Daniel. *Morley Callaghan and the Great Depression.* The Callaghan Symposium. University of Ottawa Press, 1981.

Cameron, Barry. "Rhetorical Tradition and the Ambiguity of Callaghan's Narrative Rhetoric." The Callaghan Symposium. University of Ottawa Press, 1981.

Callaghan, Barry. *Barrelhouse Kings.* Toronto: McArthur & Company, 1998.

Callaghan, Morley. *A Literary Life. Reflection and Reminiscences 1928-1990.* Holstein: Exile Editions, 2008.

Clark, O.S. *Of Toronto the Good: A Social Study.* 1898. Toronto: Coles Canadiana Collection, 1970.

Conron, Brandon. *Morley Callaghan: Critical Views on Canadian Writers, No. 10.* Toronto: McGraw-Hill Ryerson, 1975.

Edwards, Justin D. "*Strange Fugitive*, Strange City: Reading Urban Space in Morley Callaghan's Toronto." *Studies in Canadian Literature*,Volume 23.1. 1998.

Ellenwood, Ray. "Morley Callaghan, Jacques Ferron, and the Dialectic of Good and Evil." The Callaghan Symposium. University of Ottawa Press, 1981.

Marcus, Steven. "Reading the Illegible: Some Modern Representations of Urban Experience." *Visions of the Modern City: Essays in History, Art, and Literature.* Ed.

William Sharpe and Leonard Wallock. Baltimore: Johns Hopkins UP, 1987. 232-56.

Mathews, Robin. "Morley Callaghan and the New Colonialism: The Supreme Individual in Traditionless Society." *Studies in Canadian Literature* 3.1 (1978) 78-92.

McDonald, Larry. "The Civilized Ego and Its Discontents: A New Approach to Callaghan." The Callaghan Symposium. University of Ottawa Press, 1981.

McPherson, Hugo. "The Two Worlds of Morley Callaghan: Man's Earthly Quest." *Queens Quarterly*, LXIV, 3 (Autumn 1957). 350-365.

Snider, Norman. "Why Morley Callaghan Still Matters," *Globe and Mail*, 25 October, 2008.

Walsh, William. *A Manifold Voice: Studies in Commonwealth Literature.* London: Chatto & Windus, 1971.

White, Randall. *Too Good to Be True: Toronto in the 1920s.* Toronto: Dundurn, 1993.

Wilson, Edmund. *O Canada: An American's Notes on Canadian Culture.* New York: Farrar, Straus & Giroux, 1964.

Woodcock, George. "Callaghan's Toronto: The Persona of a City." *Journal of Canadian Studies* 7-2 (1972) 21-24.

Zucchi, John E. *Italians in Toronto: Development of a National Identity, 1875-1935.* Montreal: McGill-Queen's UP, 1988.

Of Interest on the Web

www.MorleyCallaghan.ca
– The official site of the Morley Callaghan Estate

www2.athabascau.ca/cll/writers/english/writers/mcallaghan.php
– Athabasca University site

www.editoreric.com/greatlit/authors/Callaghan.html
– The Greatest Authors of All Time site

www.cbc.ca/lifeandtimes/callaghan.htm
– Canadian Broadcasting Corporation (CBC) site

Exile Online Resource

www.ExileEditions.com has a section for the Exile Classics Series, with further resources for all the books in the series.

THE EXILE CLASSICS SERIES

THAT SUMMER IN PARIS (No. 1) ~ MORLEY CALLAGHAN
Memoir 6x9 247 pages 978-1-55096-688-6 (tpb) $19.95

It was the fabulous summer of 1929 when the literary capital of North America had moved to the Left Bank of Paris. Ernest Hemingway, F. Scott Fitzgerald, James Joyce, Ford Madox Ford, Robert McAlmon and Morley Callaghan... amid these tangled relationships, friendships were forged, and lost... A tragic and sad and unforgettable story told in Callaghan's lucid, compassionate prose.

NIGHTS IN THE UNDERGROUND (No. 2) ~ MARIE-CLAIRE BLAIS
Fiction/Novel 6x9 190 pages 978-1-55096-015-0 (tpb) $19.95

With this novel, Marie-Claire Blais came to the forefront of feminism in Canada. This is a classic of lesbian literature that weaves a profound matrix of human isolation, with transcendence found in the healing power of love.

DEAF TO THE CITY (No. 3) ~ MARIE-CLAIRE BLAIS
Fiction/Novel 6x9 218 pages 978-1-55096-013-6 (tpb) $19.95

City life, where innocence, death, sexuality, and despair fight for survival. It is a book of passion and anguish, characteristic of our times, written in a prose of controlled self-assurance. A true urban classic.

THE GERMAN PRISONER (No. 4) ~ JAMES HANLEY
Fiction/Novella 6x9 55 pages 978-1-55096-075-4 (tpb) $13.95

In the weariness and exhaustion of WWI trench warfare, men are driven to extremes of behaviour.

THERE ARE NO ELDERS (No. 5) ~ AUSTIN CLARKE
Fiction/Stories 6x9 159 pages 978-1-55096-092-1 (tpb) $17.95

Austin Clarke is one of the significant writers of our times. These are compelling stories of life as it is lived among the displaced in big cities, marked by a singular richness of language true to the streets.

100 LOVE SONNETS (No. 6) ~ PABLO NERUDA
Poetry 6x9 225 pages 978-1-55096-108-9 (tpb) $24.95

As Gabriel García Márquez stated: "Pablo Neruda is the greatest poet of the twentieth century – in any language." And, this is the finest translation available, anywhere!

THE SELECTED GWENDOLYN MACEWEN (No. 7)
GWENDOLYN MACEWEN
Poetry/Fiction/Drama/Art/Archival 6x9 352 pages
978-1-55096-111-9 (tpb) $32.95
"This book represents a signal event in Canadian culture." *–Globe and Mail*
The only edition to chronologically follow the astonishing trajectory of MacEwen's career as a poet, storyteller, translator and dramatist, in a substantial selection from each genre.

THE WOLF (No. 8) ~ MARIE-CLAIRE BLAIS
Fiction/Novel 6x9 158 pages 978-1-55096-105-8 (tpb) $19.95
A human wolf moves outside the bounds of love and conventional morality as he stalks willing prey in this spellbinding masterpiece and classic of gay literature.

A SEASON IN THE LIFE OF EMMANUEL (No. 9) ~ MARIE-CLAIRE BLAIS
Fiction/Novel 6x9 175 pages 978-1-55096-118-8 (tpb) $19.95
Widely considered by critics and readers alike to be her masterpiece, this is truly a work of genius comparable to Faulkner, Kafka, or Dostoyevsky. Includes 16 Ink Drawings by Mary Meigs.

IN THIS CITY (No. 10) ~ AUSTIN CLARKE
Fiction/Stories 6x9 221 pages 978-1-55096-106-5 (tpb) $21.95
Clarke has caught the sorrowful and sometimes sweet longing for a home in the heart that torments the dislocated in any city. Eight masterful stories showcase the elegance of Clarke's prose and the innate sympathy of his eye.

THE NEW YORKER STORIES (No. 11) ~ MORLEY CALLAGHAN
Fiction/Stories 6x9 158 pages 978-1-55096-110-2 (tpb) $19.95
Callaghan's great achievement as a young writer is marked by his breaking out with stories such as these in this collection... "If there is a better storyteller in the world, we don't know where he is." *–New York Times*

REFUS GLOBAL (No. 12) ~ THE MONTRÉAL AUTOMATISTS
Manifesto 6x9 142 pages 978-1-55096-107-2 (tpb) $21.95
The single most important social document in Quebec history, and the most important aesthetic statement a group of Canadian artists has ever made. This is basic reading for anyone interested in Canadian history or the arts in Canada.

TROJAN WOMEN (No. 13) ~ GWENDOLYN MACEWEN
Drama 6x9 142 pages 978-1-55096-123-2 (tpb) $19.95
A trio of timeless works featuring the great ancient theatre piece by Euripedes in a new version by MacEwen, and the translations of two long poems by the contemporary Greek poet Yannis Ritsos.

ANNA'S WORLD (No. 14) ~ MARIE-CLAIRE BLAIS
Fiction 5.5x8.5 166 pages ISBN: 978-1-55096-130-0 $19.95
An exploration of contemporary life, and the penetrating energy of youth, as Blais looks at teenagers by creating Anna, an introspective, alienated teenager without hope. Anna has experienced what life today has to offer and rejected its premise. There is really no point in going on. We are all going to die, if we are not already dead, is Anna's philosophy.

THE MANUSCRIPTS OF PAULINE ARCHANGE (No. 15)
MARIE-CLAIRE BLAIS
Fiction 5.5x8.5 324 pages ISBN: 978-1-55096-131-7 $23.95
For the first time, the three novelettes that constitute the complete text are brought together: the story of Pauline and her world, a world in which people turn to violence or sink into quiet despair, a world as damned as that of Baudelaire or Jean Genet.

A DREAM LIKE MINE (No. 16) ~ M.T. KELLY
Fiction 5.5x8.5 174 pages ISBN: 978-1-55096-132-4 $19.95
A Dream Like Mine is a journey into the contemporary issue of radical and violent solutions to stop the destruction of the environment. It is also a journey into the unconscious, and into the nightmare of history, beauty and terror that are the awesome landscape of the Native American spirit world.

THE LOVED AND THE LOST (No. 17) ~ MORLEY CALLAGHAN
Fiction 5.5x8.5 302 pages ISBN: 978-1-55096-151-5 (tpb) $21.95
With the story set in Montreal, young Peggy Sanderson has become socially unacceptable because of her association with black musicians in nightclubs. The black men think she must be involved sexually, the black women fear or loathe her, yet her direct, almost spiritual manner is at variance with her reputation.

NOT FOR EVERY EYE (No. 18) ~ GÉRARD BESSETTE
Fiction 5.5x8.5 126 pages ISBN: 978-1-55096-149-2 (tpb) $17.95

A novel of great tact and sly humour that deals with ennui in Quebec and the intellectual alienation of a disenchanted hero, and one of the absolute classics of modern revolutionary and comic Quebec literature. Chosen by the Grand Jury des Lettres of Montreal as one of the ten best novels of post-war contemporary Quebec.

STRANGE FUGITIVE (No. 19) ~ MORLEY CALLAGHAN
Fiction 5.5x8.5 242 pages ISBN: 978-1-55096-155-3 (tpb) $19.95

Callaghan's first novel – originally published in New York in 1928 – announced the coming of the urban novel in Canada, and we can now see it as a prototype for the "gangster" novel in America. The story is set in Toronto in the era of the speakeasy and underworld vendettas.

IT'S NEVER OVER (No. 20) ~ MORLEY CALLAGHAN
Fiction 5.5x8.5 190 pages ISBN: 978-1-55096-157-7 (tpb) $19.95

1930 was an electrifying time for writing. Callaghan's second novel, completed while he was living in Paris – imbibing and boxing with Joyce and Hemingway (see his memoir, Classics No. 1, *That Summer in Paris*) – has violence at its core; but first and foremost it is a story of love, a love haunted by a hanging. Dostoyevskian in its depiction of the morbid progress of possession moving like a virus, the novel is sustained insight of a very high order.

AFTER EXILE (No. 21) ~ RAYMOND KNISTER
Fiction 5.5x8.5 240 pages ISBN: 978-1-55096-159-1 (tpb) $19.95

This book collects for the first time Knister's poetry. The title *After Exile* is plucked from Knister's long poem written after he returned from Chicago and decided to become the unthinkable: a modernist Canadian writer. Knister, writing in the 20s and 30s, could barely get his poems published in Canada, but magazines like *This Quarter* (Paris), *Poetry* (Chicago), *Voices* (Boston), and *The Dial* (New York City), eagerly printed what he sent, and always asked for more – and all of it is in this book.